"I'm not going
Margaret fum

"I can't believe you expect me to marry him."
Margaret glared at Sid. "Last night, on the air,
he—" she jerked her thumb toward John "—called
me a hag."

"Mags, Mags, Mags." John got that know-it-all
gleam in his bedroom brown eyes. "I said you
looked haggard. You weren't listening again."

"Scoundrel," she said under her breath as she
moved around Sid's desk.

"Witch." John's smile was wicked as he moved in on
her.

"Reprobate." Margaret took a step closer to him,
her pulse racing while other parts of her throbbed.

"Snob."

They came together, nose to nose. Neither touched,
yet Margaret felt as if they were one. Her breasts
rose and fell rapidly as she gasped for air. The
cords in his neck became more pronounced.

From the sidelines, Sid applauded boisterously and
shouted, "Great! Just great! When you two go at it
like that, it's poetic. Ratings will skyrocket. Oh,
man, I'm so damn smart, I think I'll give myself
another raise."

Dear Reader,

We have two delightful, funny and charming
LOVE & LAUGHTER stories for you this month!
Cathie Linz concludes her MARRIAGE MAKERS
miniseries with #51 *Too Smart for Marriage,* the
story of the last remaining single Knight triplet,
Anastasia Knight. She was blessed by her fairy
godmother with a dash too much attitude and a
heck of a lot of smarts, resulting in a woman who
believes she has no use for marriage. Boy, is she
about to be proved wrong!

Then bright new talent Bonnie Tucker
continues her winning and hilarious storytelling in
#52 *Stay Tuned: Wedding at 11:00.* It brings to
mind the great classic romantic comedies like
His Girl Friday, with lots of nineties spice! Don't
miss the live, on-air wedding…maybe!

So take some time out of your busy schedule
and enjoy the lighter side of love. Remember
LOVE & LAUGHTER is 100% fat free!

Enjoy!

Malle Vallik

Malle Vallik
Associate Senior Editor

STAY TUNED: WEDDING AT 11:00

Bonnie Tucker

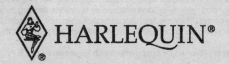

HARLEQUIN®

TORONTO • NEW YORK • LONDON
AMSTERDAM • PARIS • SYDNEY • HAMBURG
STOCKHOLM • ATHENS • TOKYO • MILAN • MADRID
PRAGUE • WARSAW • BUDAPEST • AUCKLAND

ISBN 0-373-44052-9

STAY TUNED: WEDDING AT 11:00

A funny thing happened...

Give me a slimy snake any day, but keep me far away from airplanes! Years ago, when my three-year-old daughter cried as we crossed a freeway overpass, I realized she'd inherited my fear of being in the air, sort of. To distract her, I sang out a raucous version of "Take Me Out to the Ball Game." Later that year we were on an airplane heading into Chicago. I was sitting with my hands clenched and my eyes tightly shut when my daughter asked if I was scared. I opened my eyes and nodded. In a flash, she was standing on the seat, belting out a childish version of "Take Me Out to the Ball Game." By the time she got to "It's one, two, three strikes, you're out..." with her little fists punching the air, everybody on board was laughing—including me—and the plane had landed. She bowed, then gave me a big hug. That day, I discovered fears can magically disappear when you're around someone you love. That happened to me. That happens to my heroine, Maggie St. James, in *Stay Tuned: Wedding at 11:00.*

I love to hear from my readers. Please write to me at: P.O. Box 16281, Sugar Land, Texas, 77496-6281.

—Bonnie Tucker

This is for the man
who gave me the freedom to write—
my husband, Ed.

1

AROUND THE TOWN
with Matilda Mae Tuttle
ST. JAMES AND HENNESSEY TO WED

YOU HEARD IT HERE FIRST! KSLT TV's favorite feuding coanchors of the 6:00 p.m. and 11:00 p.m. news, the brainy Margaret St. James and the devil-may-care darling and hunky John Patrick Hennessey—be still my heart—are about to set fireworks exploding off camera as well as on.

Last night during the Sugar Land Volunteer Firefighters' Chili Cook-off and Calendar-Photo Shoot, Sid Levine, KSLT's owner, let it slip to this reporter that Sugar Land's hunky darling, John, our town's most eligible bachelor, is about to become a marital statistic.

For you ladies contemplating suicide over the loss of our gorgeous fantasy man to Plain-Jane Margaret— How did she reel him in, girls?—look at the bright side. Statistically their marriage won't last long enough for the ink to dry on the license.

We'll be waiting for you, Johnny!

MARGARET ST. JAMES, with a stranglehold on the *Sugar Land Times*, made a beeline down the corridors of KSLT toward Sid Levine's office.

Hennessey—she refused to call him John because she didn't want him to get any ideas that she wanted to get *that* personal with him ever again—followed her, a pace behind, slapping his own rolled-up copy of the *Times* to his palm.

Margaret moved faster...well, as fast as any woman wearing heels and a slim straight skirt could move across tightly woven Berber carpet.

When Hennessey's shadow melted into hers she took bigger steps, not wanting any part of her, not even her shadow, to touch him. The faster she walked, the faster he walked, tossing out his flavor-of-the-day innuendo, "I like ice-queen virgins like you, Mags-of-my-heart."

"You're quite an investigative reporter, aren't you?" she said. Not that he needed to be. Sid had hired him for his godlike looks, not his journalistic skills, so she shouldn't be surprised when he didn't get his facts straight.

"I've known you a long time, Mags-of-my-heart," Hennessey said. "I've never seen evidence to the contrary."

Her stomach muscles clenched. Every ounce of her wanted to deny his taunt. If he hadn't walked out on her that one night, two years, eight months and five days ago— but who's counting?—he would've known.

Now was not the time to suggest he do his research.

With her head held high she did what she normally did when it came to dealing with the man. Ignored him. Only, being ignored didn't faze Hennessey one bit, much to her sorrow.

He spoke conversationally, not even out of breath from keeping up with her quick pace. "I'm calling my lawyer about suing Sid. Tillie Mae's column smacks of entrapment."

Entrapment? She almost laughed out loud. Hennessey couldn't possibly know what the word meant since it had over six letters.

She saw his shadow on the wall. His fist was doing the hand-jive-squeeze-oranges routine at the same time he said in his low, gravelly voice, "The faster you walk, the better it looks from back here."

She'd had enough. Margaret stopped midstride.

All six-foot-five, two hundred pounds of him rammed into her backside. "And it feels great, too," he purred seductively.

"Hen-nes-sey," she warned, not happy with the warm quivers shooting through her from the point of contact. She turned to face him. "I'll make you sorry you ever came to this station," Margaret promised, stepping away from the surge of awareness he sparked in her.

"I'm already sorry that I'm *still* at this station." His casual cocky grin didn't reach his eyes.

He'd tucked the paper under his arm. Hennessey. Solid muscle and heat.

"Listen, Mags. We've got to work together on this. It's you and me against the big guy."

"It's never been you and me against Sid," Margaret denied. "It's always been me against both of you."

"I had nothing to do with the story," he said.

She stared at him, not knowing whether or not he was telling the truth.

Finally he took his newspaper and held it up. "Okay already. If you want to believe I planted this story, fine. I hope that makes you happy. You women are all the same. You get some cockamamy idea in your head, and superglue it on your brain."

"At least I use my brain."

The smile on his lips faltered and she could swear she saw a flash of hurt in his brown eyes. It was a low blow on her part, but her stubborn pride and years of feeling as if she was second-rate in the femininity department kept her from apologizing.

"I needed a place to start, Mags," he said softly. "Whether I won this job in a game of golf against Sid, or because Sid liked the way I looked and thought my sitting next to you would help raise the ratings, doesn't matter anymore. You've been in this business long enough to know that a guy like me has to do whatever it takes to get ahead."

She lowered her gaze, not able to look into his eyes any longer, and nodded slowly. He'd been her partner on the six and eleven o'clock news for almost three years now. A long time for a man like Hennessey.

He'd never kept it a secret that he considered Sugar Land's only television station, KSLT, simply a stepping stone on his career path. He wanted to be the next Peter Jennings. He'd told her that often enough. She also knew he'd been sending out résumé tapes to every TV station in the top-ten market. And he was still here.

"I know what your problem is, Magpie." Hennessey's slow and lazy tone, and the expression on his too-handsome face turned wickedly lascivious.

"You," she answered quickly.

"Oh, Mag-o-muffin, I'm not the problem." His whiskey voice washed over her. "I'm the solution. Here for the taking." He grinned at her, his long muscular arms outstretched, exposing his massive chest and shoulders the size of a football field.

"In your dreams," she whispered.

"Don't you know it." He leaned down, closer to her face. "I've been dreaming about all the ways we can finish what we started way back then."

His firm lips were so close to her ear they grazed the outside shell. His warm, always minty breath floated down the side of her neck, tickling her skin. "Remember?" he said softly.

"Remember what?" *She remembered everything.* Her heart raced and her palms moistened as her lips clamped together hard and painfully. She gripped the *Times* with both hands now, and twisted, pretending the paper was Hennessey's neck, punishing him for making her remember a night, two years, eight months and five days ago—but who's counting?—that she wanted to forget. "You know, Hennessey, men like you—" *A man who had hurt her where she was the most vulnerable...*

"According to Matilda Mae Tuttle's column, men like me—" he flipped open to the front page "—being devil-may-care, darling and hunky are few and far between."

She tried to tell him what she thought of that column, but he held the newspaper in front of her face.

"Why argue, Magpie? I'm only quoting Tillie."

"Don't call me Magpie." Margaret flipped his paper aside. "I hate when you do that."

"If I stopped, how would you know I cared?"

"Don't care," she pleaded, walking away, wringing her *Times* and repeating her mantra, "I will get through this day as I have all others since Hennessey was forced into my life. Through persistence and patience and the ability to ignore the miscreants of society."

"Give it up, Mags," he teased from behind her. "You know you love me."

Her laugh sounded brittle, even to her own ears. "Not a chance."

They arrived at the KSLT executive offices at the same time. This was sacred ground on which no mortal man or woman dared to tread. But that didn't stop Margaret. She opened the glass door, then turned to Hennessey, who stood behind her, arrogant, and as self-confident in his manhood as she was unsure in her womanhood. "Don't embarrass me," she ordered.

Opening the door that led into Sid and Rachel's suite of offices, he grinned at her. In sympathy.

Margaret strode over the threshold, head held high, shoulders back, and forced herself not to look behind her.

SID LEVINE, owner of forty-nine percent of KSLT, spent eighty percent of his waking moments thinking of two things: golf and Hawaii. The other twenty percent he used to conjure up ways to steal control of KSLT out from under his sister, Rachel, who happened to own the other fifty-one percent. Once he was in charge, he could devote one hundred percent of his time to more important things. Like playing golf full-time after he moved to Hawaii.

If his hands weren't around the shaft of his putter, he'd have rubbed them in glee. Soon. Very soon he'd get his wish. All the players were lined up. His plan was going smoothly, and nothing, except jail if he was caught, would come between him and his goal. And he wouldn't get caught. At least not until it was too late. After all, he had listened to Mollie Bright, and took to heart the force of positive thinking.

Now, if he could only get rid of Rachel.

She was taller than him by a head, younger by ten years and with as much brown hair on her head as he lacked on his. Not that hair mattered. What *did* matter was that she drove him crazy. No amount of positive thinking could stop that, especially on days like today, when she put on that holier-than-thou attitude he despised so much, and waved Tillie Mae Tuttle's column around, causing a breeze on his green.

And there she stood, yapping at him while he tried to

concentrate on putting the golf ball in the hole. Rachel's voice was enough to get the snails in the fish tank moving.

Finally he'd had enough. "You may own two percent more of KSLT than I do, and you may be in charge of the TV station's checkbook, but you have no vision."

As far as he was concerned, not having vision was as much a sin as their stepfather making Rachel chief financial officer. If it hadn't been for Rachel holding the purse strings, he could have sold KSLT a year ago, and would not have had to resort to forgery, secrecy and deception. Not to mention a few little white lies along the way. If it hadn't been for Goody Two-shoes Rachel, he could be swinging a golf club across eighteen holes of luscious Hawaiian island green right now. Legally.

"*I* have no vision?" she repeated, slashing the paper around in the air. "Why, you sleazy, little, *old* man. Do you realize what you did when you told Tillie Mae Tuttle these lies about poor, sweet Margaret and that Casanova, John Hennessey? Do you?"

"Those aren't lies." Or they wouldn't be as soon as all the little puppets were lined up onstage with their strings ready to be pulled.

It should be obvious, even to anal-retentive Rachel, that the reason KSLT was only points away from beating Houston's CBS affiliate for the position of number-one TV station in the six o'clock time slot was because of his own tenacity. He was, after all, Sid—Man of Vision.

Sid bent at the waist, holding the putter just so, and kept his eyes focused on the little white ball. He adjusted the ball the way he liked it, with the manufacturer's imprint kissing the putting green. He was sure the ink added extra weight and the ball would roll better with the name down.

Soon, very soon, he thought, if Rachel kept her big nose out of his business, his plan would be launched.

His hands trembled slightly around the shaft. These were the weeks he'd been waiting for. He'd taken out a private post-office box, so no one at the station would get his mail. Papers were on file in Washington, D.C. All the documents had been signed on the dotted line. Sid had practiced long and hard to get Rachel's loops and swirls down right. He was sure his sister would forgive him once it was all over.

"I know you're up to no good. I can feel it in my bones."

Skinny bones, Sid thought as she looked down on him in that condescending way she had.

"Whatever little scheme you've got cooking isn't going to work."

His plan was going to work just fine. "Go back to your office and write some checks, why don't you. Leave the ideas to me."

She snapped the newspaper. "If this column is any indication of what your plans are, I'll go back to my office all right. To call our lawyer and warn him."

"Whatever makes you happy, Rach." Sid gently hit the ball, a straight easy shot, and missed the cup again. "Ah, hell, Rachel, look what you made me do." He shouldn't miss since he'd had the cup built larger than regulation size.

He retrieved his ball and placed it back on his favorite spot. "I need to concentrate," he grumbled. "Don't you have any numbers to crunch?"

"No."

"Go find some."

"I think I'll stand right here, breathe down your neck and make you miserable."

Sid heard noises coming from the reception area, saw who was walking through the glass doors and said, "Oh, sh-e-e-e-e-e-i-t."

Rachel looked, too, and finally walked away from him.

Before she left, she said, real sweetlike, "Margaret will get you."

"No one will get Sid Levine, Rachel. Remember that!" He waved the putter in the air, watched as his sister stopped Margaret near the door, then went back to his game.

2

MARGARET KNEW setting up a meeting with Sid was next to impossible. Janice, his secretary, had to schedule a time days in advance so as not to interfere with the boss's golf games, and no one, absolutely no one, got in to see him without an appointment.

In reality, no one ever got an appointment.

Coming to see Sid had been an adrenaline-induced, spur-of-the-moment decision for Margaret. And she wasn't about to let anyone get in her way. That's where Hennessey, who could always be counted on to provide a distraction, finally proved himself useful.

He had seated himself on the edge of Janice's desk, gazing into the secretary's young face and listening to her sigh, ad nauseam, "Isn't it romantic? Can I get you some coffee? I mean, you and Margaret getting married." Sigh, sigh. "Who would have thought?"

Hennessey smiled that cockeyed smile he had that initiated the sighs coming from Janice, and shrugged the famous Hennessey shrug that had women hyperventilating.

So Janice breathed faster and sighed some more and tried to work her way out of her hole. "Not that Margaret's not pretty...she really is in that queenlike kind of way she has. But you and her? I mean, well...she's really smart."

"You think I'm not?" He smiled charmingly, but cringed.

"No...no...I didn't meant that." Janice's eyes widened and she quickly backtracked. "Of course you're smart. How about a doughnut, John? Corned beef on rye?"

"That's okay, Janice." At her doubtful expression he tried to reassure her again. "Really, relax."

John understood very well how women felt when they complained about being judged, and treated, by the way they looked. Mags was slender and regal, had gone to Rice University, and before coming back to Sugar Land, she'd worked in the big TV market, WLS in Chicago. Everyone around here was in awe of her and treated her with respect.

He, on the other hand, never graduated from high school, instead earning his GED several years after he'd quit. On top of that, he looked like some ski instructor or football player with more brawn than brains.

When people talked to Mags, they spoke in hushed, respectful tones. When they talked to him, they talked louder, slower, as if they thought he was too dumb to understand what they had to say.

The constant need to prove himself was wearing on him. He wasn't dumb. He'd just had a few hard knocks is all.

He glanced to his side and saw Mags looking at him, a look of pity all over her face. Damn. He didn't want or need her to feel sorry for him. He'd been fighting his own demons for a long time, and he didn't need her sympathy.

Margaret heard Janice's comments to Hennessey, saw the hurt expression flash across his face, then disappear behind his ever-present toothpaste-commercial grin, and wanted to slap the girl for being so insensitive. Not even Hennessey deserved to listen to some little ninny prattle on about his shortcomings. If anyone was going to prattle, it would be Margaret.

Anyway, it wasn't Hennessey's fault he'd gotten the job because Sid thought his looks would raise the ratings. It was only his fault that he *took* the job.

Hennessey's muscular body seemed to relax, and he continued to let Janice chatter, the babbling giving Margaret a chance to make it to Sid's office unobserved. She'd have to remember to thank Hennessey someday for turning the normally stalwart Janice into an unthinking mass of mush.

Margaret had almost reached Sid's doorway when Rachel came rushing through, almost knocking her down.

"I refuse to believe this," Rachel declared as she slapped her *Times* on Margaret's copy.

"I should hope so," Margaret replied.

"You'll take care of it then."

"That's why I'm here to see Sid."

"I'm counting on you." Rachel patted Margaret's arm. "Good luck. You'll need it dealing with him."

She watched Rachel surge down the corridor, then turned and entered the inner sanctum.

Sid looked up from his squatting position over a golf ball and moaned melodramatically. "What did I ever do to deserve the kind of aggravation you women are giving me?"

"Here's some more aggravation for you today. I quit."

Sid stood and swung. Hard. The ball missed the cup, hit the wall, ricocheted back and slammed into the front of his leg. "This is all your fault," he accused, hopping in a circle, clutching the club and his wounded knee together.

"Did you hear what I said?"

"I'm crippled, no thanks to you. Not deaf." He limped toward his desk, using the club as a cane. "You can't quit."

"I just did."

"Sit down, darling. Let's discuss this."

"There's nothing to discuss."

Sid eased himself behind the desk no one, not even Janice, was allowed to breathe on. Lined neatly across the top were stacks of pamphlets and brochures divided alphabetically by the location of exotic Hawaiian country-club golfing resorts and condos. Each no doubt beckoned to Sid and his money, calling out, "Buy me, buy me."

Margaret tossed the *Times* across the stacks of brochures. They toppled into each other. "How dare you tell those lies to Tillie Mae Tuttle!"

"What lies?" Sid put two fingers on the edge of the newspaper she'd hurled at him and started to lift.

Her hand smacked down, anchoring the paper in place. "Move it and you're a dead man."

"The trouble with you brainy types, Margaret, is you only see one side of an issue."

"There *is* only one side—the side of truth, justice and the Texas way."

"There you go spouting the U. S. of A. Constitution again."

Margaret blew out an exasperated breath. "Sid, what in the world possessed you? Why did you tell Tillie Mae that I'm getting married to *it* out there?" She tossed her head in the direction of the reception area.

"Why don't you sit down, darling?" He pointed to a chair at the opposite side of the room, the one farthest away from him.

The only part of her that moved was an arching eyebrow.

"I'll explain everything and you'll understand," Sid promised.

"I don't know what kind of idea you've cooked up this time, but it's not going to work. Everyone on this planet knows how I feel about *him*." Hennessey, who made her feel like a failure as a woman. And now Sid had started a rumor about them getting married. Just knowing that Hennessey found her undesirable, unattractive and plain made this whole marriage rumor the ultimate humiliation. Marriage between them would never—could never happen. She knew that even if Hennessey was in the market for a bride, which he'd always made clear to everyone he wasn't, he'd never pick her. As if she'd want him to, she thought scornfully.

"Of course it'll work, darling. Leave it to me."

"Leave it to you?" She almost choked.

Sid's cheesy grin turned gleeful. "That's exactly what I'm counting on."

JOHN TWISTED his head a little away from Janice so he could watch Mags through Sid's doorway. Ever since the night he'd walked out of her house, and out of her private life, which was the hardest thing he'd ever done, he found himself spending hours watching her, wondering if his pride was too big, his ego too vulnerable. He'd never know now what might have happened if only he'd listened to his heart. Instead, he'd deferred to his common sense, which told him that a man with nothing didn't make love to a woman who had everything.

Mags was and always would be a St. James, a woman of privilege and power. A woman who could work any-where in the world and name her price.

He'd always be a Hennessey, a nobody. No one came offering him jobs, unless Mags came attached to the deal.

Well, he'd saved his pride, all right. Also got himself a few other things he hadn't bargained on in the process. Mags in a three-year woman-thing snit, and himself a frus-trated mass of male testosterone. No wonder the viewers tuned in to watch them every night. He and Mags were two bodies ready to explode.

Still, he'd have to have a talk with that Tillie Mae Tuttle for calling his little Magpie a plain Jane. She was anything but, especially from the viewpoint he was looking at now.

"Johnny!" Sid bellowed. "Get your butt in here."

John never had taken orders well. He walked slowly into the office, concentrating on watching Mags's bottom wav-ing in the air to the beat of the finger she had pointed at Sid's nose.

He stopped at the opposite side of the desk. Never one to stand when he could sit, and not one to sit in a chair that would place him lower than those whose salaries were more substantial than his, he sat himself down on the edge of the desk. With one foot on the floor and one leg hanging over the side, he peered down at his boss.

"Get the hell off there." Sid's complexion blotched as he prodded John with the end of his putter, which John easily knocked away.

Mags finally straightened, both to John's relief and dismay. She pointed to the newspaper still spread across the desk. "Explain this. Now," she said, and plunked herself down on the other side of Sid's desk.

"It's easy," Sid said, giving John the evil eye. "It's all about money and the sweeps period and advertising. You know, big bucks. Dollars. Lots of George Washingtons. Simple."

"I'm aware of the concept," Mags told him. "But what does advertising have to do with this article?"

"Why don't you both go sit over there?" Again Sid pointed to the opposite side of the room.

Neither John nor Mags moved.

"All right, all right." Sid let out a rattling breath. "Marriage equals dollars. You'll get married on the six o'clock news. But before that, I have a plan for the whole week leading up to the big day. By the time you get back here…"

"Back here?" Mags asked.

"I'll explain later. The wedding next week will push us to number one in the six o'clock spot."

"Well, Sid," Mags said sarcastically. "Why six? Why not during the eleven o'clock news?"

"You're kidding. I can't miss my 'Nick at Night.'"

"We're not doing this. You couldn't have believed that we'd go along with this crazy scheme." Her face had turned a delicate shade of pink and her hands were clenched so hard the knuckles had turned white.

"Sure you will."

Her head shook.

"You know, kids, I'm just as upset about this mess with Matilda as you are. The scoop was supposed to break on KSLT's very own 'Sugar Land This Morning' show. You can blame the leak on jalapeños."

"You're crazy," John and Mags said at the same time.

Sid gaped at both of them. "You two agreeing about something? That can't happen."

"Sid…" Mags got that warning tone in her voice John

knew so well. While it didn't affect him, he noticed Sid cringe. "Your point?"

"I'm getting to it." He rubbed the shaft of the club. "Last night, there I was, doing my civic duty like I do every year, in the Sugar Land Firefighters' Chili Cook-off and Calendar-Photo Shoot, minding my own business, stirring my sweet and mild chili—"

"He's changing the subject again," John interrupted. "I think I'll hide his tee-times." He opened the top drawer of the desk and started rummaging. Sid slammed the drawer shut, missing John's fingers by millimeters.

"I was minding my own business—which you'd better do, Johnny-boy—having a simple, private discussion with Cindy Meadows, the guest host of 'Sugar Land This Morning.' I was stirring up the beans and meat, giving her the confidential scoop about your wedding when along comes Matilda."

"There's no wedding," Mags snapped.

Sid waved an arm at her. "Now, Margaret, do you want to hear the story or not?"

John caught Mags rolling her eyes. He would have thought she'd have gotten up and left by now, but she sat right there, waiting for Sid to finish. He had to feel a little bit smug. The idea of marriage between them, no matter how improbable, had her sitting on the edge of Sid's desk. She looked real anxious. As anxious as he bet their viewers would be to see them when they broadcast the news tonight.

Sid became even more animated. "Matilda hands me what I thought was a green pepper. It looked like a green pepper. It was shaped like a green pepper. She tells me it's the sweetest little hybrid pepper I'll ever eat. So when she says I should try it, and if I like it I can add it to my chili recipe and that the pepper can be the secret ingredient that will make my chili win the cook-off, I believed her.

"So, I took a bite, a big bite, and damned if the thing didn't turn out to be a Texas-size jalepeño. That woman tricked me. *Me!* My eyes teared up, like a baby, for heaven's sakes. My nose was dripping, my head was sweating, my mouth was on fire. I begged Matilda. 'Water,' I said. 'Water.' But she held out on me until I gave her the complete story.''

"There's no story," Mags said through closed teeth.

"Of course there is. I gave it to Tillie Mae. Blackmailers don't put me in a very good mood, Margaret, so don't go all huffy on me. That woman scooped KSLT with our own news.''

"There's no scoop." John settled more comfortably on the desk, and grinned at Sid's horrified expression when the wood creaked. "Have you been nipping into the whiskey you keep hidden in your bottom drawer?''

"How'd you know about that?'' Sid ranted.

"More like the jalepeño burned his brain," Mags said, grunting.

John liked it when she did her girly grunt. He liked her little throaty sounds. Then she put her hands, fingers drumming, on those great hipbones of hers. In that tight skirt, he could see the outline of her long thighs and the rounded place where her knees hid under the material. He slanted his head slightly to get a better view of a curvy calf and trim ankle.

She tilted her head. Her aristocratic nostrils flared, those high cheekbones blossomed with rosy color and those blue eyes shot him daggers.

Maybe he shouldn't have gotten so self-righteous three years ago. He winked at her, which made the rest of her face turn the same color as her cheekbones. Still hot. He finally turned back to Sid. "What possessed you?''

Sid pointed the putter at Mags's behind. "The devil made me do it.''

"You're so wormy," she told him.

"I may be a worm, but when the November ratings come out, I'll be the happiest worm in Sugar Land.''

Margaret wouldn't go down without a fight. Her reputation was at stake here. There was no way she'd get dragged into some lie that would cause her to lose not only credibility with her viewers, but her self-respect.

She pointed a threatening, bloodred-tipped finger at Sid. "You'll be lucky if we both don't sue you."

Sid leaned his head back, a sly grin plastered on his face. "You can't sue me," he gloated. "I've got a signed employment contract that says so. To paraphrase. Clause twelve—No suing allowed. You know, sometimes you amaze me, Margaret. I'd think for a sigma cuma lauder—"

"She's only a cuma lauder, Sid," Hennessey corrected. "Even I knew that."

"It's summa cum laude." She knew they purposely never got it right.

"Sigma, summa, alpha, whatsa, who cares?" Sid brushed them both off with a wave of his hand.

"You know, Sid," Margaret said softly. "When your stepfather—may he rest in peace, and *not* be turning over in his grave because he's watching what you're doing—ran KSLT, this station was a place of distinction. Now it's one of degradation, which I can pinpoint to a time three years ago, the exact moment you let *that* beat you in golf." She waved her hand in Hennessey's direction. "And back then my summa carried a lot of weight around here."

"The six o'clock news is number two in the ratings." Hennessey glared at her, forcing Margaret to look into his face, to see his anger, and something else.

His voice filled with barely contained rage, and she knew he was trying to rein in his emotions.

"You and I both know," he said, "that until I sat at the anchor desk next to you, my little Magpie, your newscast was in last place."

He pushed himself off the desk, scowling. "Without me you'd still be in last place. So I'm choosing to ignore the insults you swing in my direction, because I'm bigger than that, Magpie. Only *you* better remember that until I came along, your cumma, sigma, gotcha, whatever, wasn't going to save KSLT from the direction it was going—bankruptcy.''

''I don't know what you're talking about.'' But she knew and it hurt. She'd never had the success her accomplishments deserved. For all her experience in news broadcasting, for all the awards she'd won, like the IRIS, for the documentary she'd written, produced and directed. Once, *Public Schools, Private Lies* aired, and immediately changes in the Chicago public-school system were implemented. Then there was the Press Club award she garnered the same year she'd left Chicago. There were more awards, too, but none of that mattered here in Sugar Land. She hadn't been able to pull the ratings up.

Then Hennessey and his to-die-for body, his movie-star looks and his overdone charm joined her on the anchor desk. And their ratings began to soar.

''For a summa—'' he said the word like a curse ''—you're dense.''

''Dense?'' she said, hopping off the desk.

Hennessey gave her one of his famous pretty-boy smirks. ''Don't you understand the word *dense* or is it too common?''

Margaret turned back to Sid as if he had some control over Hennessey. ''Last night Mr. Vocabulary over there called me a tight-ass, on the air in front of thousands of viewers. Where are the censors?''

''Are you saying KSLT doesn't have any censors on the payroll?'' Sid asked.

''Do I have to put up with this? The night before he called me a hag.''

''Mags, Mags, Mags.'' Hennessey got that know-it-all gleam in his bedroom brown eyes, and used the smoky voice he used, the one that made her arms tingle. ''I said you looked haggard. You weren't listening again.''

''Scoundrel,'' she said softly, moving around the desk.

''Witch.'' His smile was wicked as he moved in on her.

''Reprobate.'' She took a step closer to him.

"Snob."

"Wastrel."

"Prude."

"Libertine."

"Miss Priss."

They came together, nose-to-nose, their breaths tangling, getting caught in their words. Neither touched, yet she felt as if they were so tightly woven not even Sid's putter could slice them apart. Her pulse was racing, and parts of her were throbbing. Her breasts rose and fell rapidly as she gasped for air. The cords in his neck became more pronounced.

From the sidelines, Margaret heard Sid applaud boisterously, and shout, "Great! Just great! Oh man, oh man, I'm so damn smart I think I'll give myself another raise."

Gradually the tension in Margaret's shoulders eased and her breathing slowed. Finally she turned away from Hennessey and his laughing Irish eyes, his wavy brown hair and the kissed-by-the-gods handsomeness that left most women—but not her since she'd taken the Hennessey antibiotic—stuttering, gasping, panting and stripping.

Sid crowed, "When you two go at it like that, it's poetic. Magic. Ratings will skyrocket. Our advertising rates will triple. I'm counting on you to keep it up now. Don't get soft on each other, especially during the next eight to ten days."

Margaret tried to concentrate on what Sid had said, but concentrating was hard with Hennessey standing so close to her, breathing her air, cutting into her space. Their shoulders touched through cloth, the omnipotent power of his presence torched her. His size alone made her feel small, even though in heels she stood five foot eight.

He turned his head toward her and caught her staring. She quickly turned the other way, but not before she saw he wore the same sexy, womanizing grin he used on the air. The one that made women mail him their underwear.

She put her hand over her racing heart, reminding herself she was immune to his grin.

"You two are beautiful." Sid kissed his fingers then waved them toward the ceiling. "Even you, Margaret. So don't look at me like that. You're the hottest pair since Scarlett and Rhett. Tracy and Hepburn. Miss Piggy and Kermit."

"Miss Piggy?"

"I can go with Kermit," Hennessey said. "As long as I can kiss Miss Piggy." He looked at Margaret. "How 'bout it. I love the way your tail curls."

Margaret slid into a chair on the other side of Sid's desk, shaking her head in frustration.

Sid expounded, "You've already burned up the TV tubes from here to the state capital."

"I don't think TVs have tubes anymore," Hennessey said, then bent down and whispered, tickling Margaret's ear, "Why don't you stop by my house sometime and we can test my tubular theory together? For old times' sake."

Margaret's face overheated, her heart banged in her chest and her palms turned to ice. "Oh, please..."

"I aim to." Hennessey made it a seductive promise.

Sid bounced up and down in his chair. "I love it, I love it! Next Friday, November twenty-seventh, you two will be happily wed, right there on the six o'clock news. By the time sweeps period is over, KSLT will be in first place. Take that—" he shot a fist in the air "—CBS."

"Sid, retract the story." Margaret wasn't above begging. "Your whole scheme's unethical."

"Since when is there ethics in the news?" Sid asked, surprise in his voice. "Did you ever hear me say that, Margaret?"

"No," she admitted.

He turned to Hennessey. "Did you?"

"Not me."

"So what's the problem?"

"All right, Sid, you've had your fun, but the fun stops

here,'' Margaret said. "I won't be a part of this lie. I have no intention of being linked romantically with Hennessey. He's only my partner on the air, and I put up with that grudgingly. That's as far as my relationship with him goes.''

"What lie? At the end of sweeps week, you'll be married. That's no lie. When Tiny Tim married Miss whatever-her-name-was, on Johnny Carson, the show's ratings soared.''

"Miss Vicki," John supplied.

Grinning like a proud father, Sid said, "Look how smart our own Johnny is.''

Only generations of good breeding kept Margaret sitting still. Sid, the pitiful man, was out to ruin her. She wouldn't let that happen.

Sid leaned back in his chair. "You'll have the best wedding my money can buy. Wait till I tell you the plans.''

Margaret jerked upright, her eyes widened at the sudden realization that her mother had most likely read the *Times* this morning, and was already planning the wedding.

"Sid, do you realize what you've done? My mother…''

"What about Myrna?" Panic and fear were evident in his voice.

Sid had every reason to be scared of Myrna, especially if he was up to no good, which he was. No one messed around with her mother and lived a pleasant life afterward. The series of events Tillie's article had probably set off in Margaret's family made her groan. Long. Loudly.

When she'd read Tillie's column this morning, the first thing she should have done, right after she spewed hot coffee all over her robe and cleaned up the mess, was to call her mother and tell her the article wasn't true.

Margaret should have remembered the engraved proto-type of a fill-in-the-groom's-name wedding announcement she and her sister, Essie, had been given that Valentine's Day twenty years ago. She knew the words by heart.

Myrna Loy and Dr. Randolph St. James
are pleased to announce the engagement
of their daughter
Margaret "Tootie" O'Brien St. James
to ———————.
Tootie is the granddaughter of
Clara Bow and Jordan Mann
and the great-granddaughter of
Lillian Gish and the late Harold Gish.

Margaret should count herself lucky that Hennessey's malignant nicknames had been limited to Mags and Magpies. Innocent stuff. By tomorrow, he'd be in possession of *real* ammunition, when the inevitable newspaper announcement came out.

She loved her family. It wasn't her fault they were all a little kooky. She was sure every family in America had one or two silly quirks. Hers happened to be that everyone was named after a movie star.

Her mother loved the movie *Meet Me In St. Louis* and had named her Margaret O'Brien, after the actress who played Tootie in the movie. Her sister had been christened Judy Garland, and nicknamed Essie.

Margaret knew there would be an announcement in the paper, too, because her mother was nothing if not efficient. That wedding announcement had probably been filled in and faxed to the *New York Times,* the *Houston Chronicle, Texas Monthly* and every other society columnist in Texas, New York, Los Angeles, London, Paris and Milan, most of whom Myrna knew personally.

Then there was the most important newspaper of all. In Dallas. Myrna had a thing against Dallas society, and would like nothing more than to rub her daughter's marriage into the faces of those women she'd shared Greek letters with at Southern Methodist University.

What a joke. Poor Myrna. She had such hope for her firstborn daughter. Margaret hated to break the news to her

mother that even if Hennessey wanted to marry her, which
he didn't, he never would. Hennessey didn't find her ap-
pealing, attractive or desirable. She, Margaret St. James,
had a successful career. But she was a failure at womanhood.

Margaret would have wept if she were a weepy type of
person. Since she wasn't, she moaned painfully under the
stress and aggravation sure to come. Even Hennessey
looked at her with a worried twist to his lips.

Right now, though, all Margaret knew was that after
growing up being called Tootie by friends, family, teachers
and schoolmates, Hennessey calling her Mags seemed
pretty darn good.

"Margaret," Sid barked. "Get your head off your lap
and take it like a man. Forget your mother. I have. Think
ratings. Hey, you two haven't done *it,* have you?" For the
second time in less than a minute Sid looked worried.

"Oh, really, Sid," Margaret croaked as her insides began
to shiver with the memory of how close they had once
come to doing *it.* "Me and him? Come on."

"And once you're married I order you not to do *it* then,
either. Not to do *it* ever."

"Sid—" Margaret tried to cut in, then stopped. What
would she say? That they had almost done *it,* but Hennessey had found her lacking and left her before they started?
Even if they did marry, Hennessey would be more inclined
to walk out on their wedding night rather than do *it* with
her. She pinched the underside of her arm, relishing the
slight pain. She had to get her mind off those morbid
thoughts. She wasn't that pitiful.

"Don't argue with me about this. My plan is that you
two get married, and next February, which I timed perfectly
for the next sweeps period, KSLT will announce on the air
that you and lover-boy are nuptially unfit."

"What do you mean 'unfit'?" Hennessey asked.

"That you've never consummated. You know, that
means that you don't…" Sid made lewd hand gestures.

"And that way you can get divorced with no problem. On the air, of course. Remember February. Pencil in the month on your calendars."

"No one's going to believe that story," Hennessey stated matter-of-factly. "I'm known for my consummating."

He may be known for that, but not with her.

She would put from her mind, once and for all, memories of that one night, two years, eight months and five days ago—but she wasn't counting—when she'd lain next to him and known his touch. The feel of his masculine heat and muscles, tendons and skin, brawn and power. To even think that she might feel him touching her again was absolutely the most ridiculous thought imaginable.

He didn't want her. She pinched herself again. No...no...no, *she* didn't want him.

He would never know how it felt to have her flesh stroked against his, to have their naked legs—his rough, hers silky—tangle together. She knew hers were silky, too, because she used Knowing body cream and dusting powder every single day, and night, without fail. It would be his loss that he would never know the softness of her skin, or smell the dusky-sweet fragrance she rubbed into all the parts of her body hidden underneath a bra and panty hose.

And the very idea of his masculinity intimately entwined with her femininity—well, he'd had his chance once, and he'd blown it.

Not only was the whole marriage scheme Sid had plotted out a bad fantasy, she simply wasn't interested in Hennessey. Not anymore. Not at all. Not ever again. Period. End of story.

Margaret squirmed back in the chair, not finding release from the tension swirling from stomach to groin. She took her *Times* off Sid's desk and used it to fan her hot face.

The stress from working with Sid and Hennessey would kill her yet.

3

"UNCONSUMMATED MARRIAGES are grounds for an annulment, not a divorce," Margaret corrected them, brushing aside wisps of hair the newspaper had blown in her eyes.

Hennessey, with his male chest expanded like a peacock, boasted, "As long as I'm around, no marriage goes unconsummated."

She wiped beads of moisture off her forehead and turned away from his— What would a person call a statement like that? A promise?

Sid's eyebrows met together like neighbors across a picket fence. "Margaret's a respectable woman. So you make sure you keep that zipper of yours zipped. She's not one of your everyday broads needing consummating."

"Sid, your chauvinistic tendencies are showing," she stated.

"All right. You're a special broad. Now are you happy?"

She stopped fanning. "You're a sick man."

Sid put a hand to his forehead. "No, I'm feeling fine. How 'bout you, Johnny-boy? You doing okay?"

"Couldn't be better."

Margaret's gaze flew right back to Hennessey. He was actually enjoying this whole show. When was he going to do his share and give Sid a dose of reality? Why did she always have to do all the work?

Sid puffed out his beer belly, and said expansively, "Now for the big moment you've all been waiting for— my wedding gift. I've decided to give you something so special, you'll have no doubt how much I appreciate the cooperation you've shown me. You're going to love it.''

She doubted it. Sid's idea of a gift for every occasion was a box of one dozen golf balls with his photograph imprinted on each ball. She'd gotten Sid's golf balls for Christmas, Sid's golf balls for her birthday and Sid's golf balls for her five-year anniversary with KSLT. She did not want to see any of Sid's balls ever again.

"You two have turned out to be real team players," Sid said expansively. "I'm rewarding your sacrifices. Johnny, this gift is not only for the wedding, but also for taking the news that you'll have to remain abstinent until February, like a real man."

"I didn't agree to anything." He looked over at Margaret, giving her that sexy Hennessey look.

"Saintly, that's what you are, Johnny-boy. Damned saintly."

"Sid—" Hennessey tried to cut in.

"And Margaret, this gift is also for not clawing my eyes out, or zinging your mother, Myrna—lovely woman—on me when you found out you'll have to put up with Johnny's saintliness."

"I don't have to put up with anything. Right now I'm this close—" she put two fingertips together and held them up "—to going on the air tonight and blowing the whole story." The competitive, unscrupulous, lying cur. She stuck her nose as high up in the air as it would go. St. Jameses for generations back would have been proud.

"Oh no you don't," Hennessey retorted. "You don't have the market on self-righteousness. I'm blowing the story first."

Sid ignored the comment, and turned to her. "Margaret, sit down," he ordered. "You have a contract with this station, and even though John doesn't, he's not leaving this room, either."

Hennessey's expression had flashed quickly from militant to stricken when Sid mentioned contracts. She would have missed the look of dejection on his face if she hadn't been trained to read people.

Sid wheeled his chair around and opened the door to the credenza behind his desk.

"All my contract says is that I need to perform my job for the good of the station," Margaret said.

"Exactly. And that's what you're going to do." Sid pulled out three boxes and placed them on his desk.

"I knew it. Golf balls," Margaret said with disdain. The day had gone from bad to worse. And she had a feeling it would be downhill from here. "You do know, don't you, that every New Year's Day your sister, Rachel, organizes all your loyal employees for a game of miniature golf," she said sweetly. "Then we all meet at Jinx Links and practice swinging at your precious balls."

"My commemorative face balls?" His black eyes bulged right out of their sockets. He even stopped arranging the boxes on his desk. "Are you telling me they don't keep those balls as a testimonial to their days here at KSLT? They don't put them in a place of honor on a shelf, or in a display cabinet?"

"No."

"They don't take them home and arrange them in the dining-room hutch along with the good dishes?"

"Oh, please." She put her elbow on the arm of the chair, resting her chin in the palm of her hand.

"I had no idea. I want a list of the people who're whacking at my balls."

She pointed at Hennessey.

"Hey," he said. "I only hit at your face twice."

"Never mind all that. I'll take care of the staff next month at Christmas-bonus time."

"What bonus?" Hennessey asked. "I never got a bonus."

"And you never will," Sid said. "Let's get back to my balls. These balls are for the important people, and you're going to deliver them for me." Sid arranged the three boxes in a triangle. "From this moment on, the conversation we're about to have is confidential and off the record. It's to go no further than these four walls. Is that understood?"

Hennessey shrugged. "I suppose."

"Margaret?"

"It all depends."

"Well, that's good enough for me." Sid settled back into his chair. "Two big corporations, Cuddle Me Clothing and Fabulous Fat-Free Foods are both considering sinking big advertising dollars into the station during your 6:00 p.m. newscasts. Maybe even the 11:00 p.m., but that's not firm yet. The numbers aren't there. You're still trailing behind Leno and Letterman."

"So what's the secret?" Margaret asked.

"The secret is that both companies have two conditions that have to be met before they'll commit."

After a pistachio-nut moment of silence, Hennessey finally cracked. "What are they?"

"I'm glad you asked that, Johnny-boy. The first is that the owners of Fabulous Fat-Free Foods and Cuddle Me Clothing want to meet you and Margaret. The second thing is that the 6:00 p.m. news has to be in first place before they'll advertise. And they don't want anyone else to know that they're bidding on time."

"Are they crazy?" she asked.

"No, Margaret. They're from New York."

"I don't get it," Hennessey said. "Why the secrecy?"

Sid leaned closer, and whispered, "If our other advertisers get wind of this deal, they'll try to lock in the rates they have now before our ratings go up, leaving no room to sell time to the New York companies at higher prices. And Rachel, being the shallow-minded businesswoman she is—I don't know why my stepdad handed her the purse strings—would sell to our advertisers at the lower rates. So everything is top secret. Especially from my sister. Understand?"

"You can't do that, Sid," Margaret said. "It's as unethical as your planting the story about Hennessey and me. You're trying to swindle the advertisers.''

"You're all so damn naive. TV stations do crap like this all the time," Sid shouted. "It's not up to either of you to question my judgment. Now pay attention. I'm getting to the complicated part. There's still a little more than a week left of the sweeps period. So, guess where you two are going? Here's a hint. Think wedding present and Johnny's going to love it.''

"I'm not going anywhere," Margaret muttered. "I have commitments here.''

Sid ignored her, and said, "The Big Apple. The town that never sleeps. I'm giving my favorite love-doves—that's you two in case you don't recognize yourselves—an all-expense-paid trip to New York City. I bought you the best coach seats on the plane.''

"Plane?" Margaret's mouth dropped open. "Do you mean airplane?''

"How else?''

"You're sending us to New York?" Hennessey sounded reverent.

"Why?" she demanded.

"Haven't you been listening? The owners of Cuddle Me Clothing and Fabulous Fat-Free Foods want to meet you. So, because I'm the generous kind of guy that I am, I'm sending you off today. With an unlimited expense account up to a thousand dollars.''

Hennessey had a giant grin slapped across his face. "We're really going to New York? As in right now?''

"That's right.''

"I'm not going on an airplane." Margaret crossed her arms in front of her, daring Sid to tangle with a St. James.

"How do you think you'll be getting there, Margaret? On a bird?" Sid laughed, fluttering his hands like wings. "No need for both of you to thank me at once.''

This couldn't be happening to her. She, who wasn't

afraid of anything, was terrified to fly. Five years ago she'd had a vision…

"What time's our plane?" Hennessey looked as if he was having a hard time containing his excitement.

"It takes off at three this afternoon. Gives you time to prerecord the 'In Your Face' spot for the news tonight, get home, throw some clothes in a bag and head out to the airport. Then it's four days of wining and dining at the expense of the other guys. Couldn't be better if I'd planned it myself. What am I saying? I did!"

"I'm not going." Margaret shook her head and a finger, too. Her audience of two weren't paying attention. "I'm not going!" She spoke louder and more forcibly. "I told you when you hired me that I wouldn't fly anywhere. Sid, you agreed that I wouldn't have to travel in this job when you hired me. We shook on it."

"Oh, hell, Margaret," Sid taunted. "You didn't get that in writing. A handshake's only good until you wash your hands. Anyway, if you read your contract, you'll see that you're required to do whatever the hell I tell you to do."

"Where does it say that? Show me."

"Don't get technical. I hate it when you get technical."

"Hennessey can go himself. That's what he wants anyway." In her most superior tone, the one she used when her sister's dog wet on her carpet, she said, "Everyone knows, Sid, that if God wanted women to fly, he'd have given them wings."

Sid pointed a stubby finger at her, smiling as he threatened, "You don't have a choice in the matter. This is my wedding gift and you'll take it whether you like it or not. And you'll be grateful and thank me. Understand!"

Margaret's bottom lip began to quiver, but the tears of helpless frustration didn't fall. She flew off the chair and walked around the desk until she stood right next to Sid, purposefully invading his space.

Hennessey stood behind her, singing a baritone, off-key rendition of "New York, New York."

"Let's be reasonable about this, okay, Sid?" she said. "Let's talk like grown-ups. Can you do that?"

"Don't get all uppity on me."

"I'm sorry. But it would save you money—you like money—if you flew all those New York corporate people here."

"Impossible."

"Why?"

"I get a bigger tax write-off with you going there. Besides, your fans are going to love it. Margaret and John on their New York adventure."

Margaret sighed despondently and looked out the window. The sun was too bright today. She was sure sunny weather wasn't good for flying. Mirages in the airspace. Pilots with scratched sunglasses. Pilots with cataracts caused by too many ultraviolet rays and megadoses of vitamin D. Pilots didn't care about how bad it was to fly on a sunny day. They'd fly no matter what.

John knew Mags didn't have any desire to leave Sugar Land. She'd already worked in the Chicago market, and had been pretty successful there before quitting and coming back to her hometown. He didn't know why she gave it all up. If it had been him, he would have continued up the ladder until he'd reached the highest rung—New York City.

But it hadn't been him, and he hadn't had the kind of opportunities she'd had.

Now he'd been given an opportunity to prove to everyone he could make it with the big boys. He wasn't about to let Mags stand in his way.

"I know this will be a great sacrifice," John said, keeping a straight face. "But I'll make it in this case. Sid, I'll go myself."

If he could get to New York, alone, and meet with the networks, without Mags there to undermine him, whether she meant to or not, he could prove how good he really was without her.

He looked at her. She was looking back at him, her eyes

filled with such heartfelt gratitude that he almost felt bad that he'd made the offer to go alone out of pure selfishness. Then she smiled slightly, and his heart tightened.

Sid bellowed, "Impossible. I made the deal. Either you both go, or neither one of you go."

Her shoulders drooped. Poor, poor Mags, John thought. If he were any kind of man, he would have told Sid that neither one of them would be going. She looked that terrified. He wanted to do that for her, he really did.

But he couldn't. The city of New York had just been placed within his reach. He could no more turn down the opportunity to meet with those network people who had been sitting on his résumé tapes for the past few months, than he could voluntarily stop breathing.

His need to succeed had become all-consuming. He had to prove wrong all those who'd told him he'd always be a nobody. Mostly, he had to prove it to himself.

Still, he was surprised at how powerful the urge to help Mags was, and more surprised at how hard he had to work at stopping himself from standing up to Sid for her, and refusing to make the trip.

Then, too, there were other urges he'd had to suppress when it came to Mags. When she had that militant look on her face, he got excited. And hard. There was no accounting for the reaction he had to her. That he'd always had to her. Three years ago when he'd had the chance, he probably should have let his male pride and ego go to hell. Instead, he'd walked out on her.

John grabbed the putter out of Sid's hand and went to the green, half listening, half watching as Mags tried to convince Sid to change his mind, with no luck.

He gripped the putter tight, a reaction to the shaky-lip thing Mags did. When that bottom lip trembled the way it did now, he got even harder than when she did her drill-sergeant routine. Now *that* wasn't rational. What man went hard when a woman's bottom lip started to shake? Only him. And since he knew how he reacted to her, why did he keep staring at her, watching that lip, torturing himself?

Hell, if he ever found the answer, maybe he'd understand why every night on the air he made sure he ticked her off just enough to get that lip moving.

When John caught Mags looking at him, he gave her a cocky half grin and went back to practicing his putting.

Margaret knew she'd lost Sid's attention, not that she'd ever really had it, as soon as Hennessey took the putter and walked over to the green. Sid never could resist watching Hennessey hit the ball. She could understand why. Hennessey had the physique of a natural athlete, all steel muscle, delineated and sculpted. She watched as he gently tapped the ball and sent it on its way into the cup. He made everything look so easy.

"Hey, Johnny, how'd you do that?" Sid abandoned Margaret and rushed over to Hennessey, giving her a chance to have a semiprivate nervous breakdown.

Finally giving up on the breakdown—no one in her family ever broke down—Margaret followed Sid, not yet willing to abandon the idea that she might convince him to come to his senses about this whole marriage, New York, illegal scheme he'd cooked up. "Sid, did you listen to anything I said? Sid? Sid? Hennessey?"

She may as well have been talking to one solid brick wall and one termite-infested fence. She watched both men bending over the golf ball as if they hadn't a worry in the world.

Hennessey looked up when she hadn't expected him to, captured her gaze and held up a second golf ball before placing it on the AstroTurf.

"You want to know how I got the ball in the cup with one smooth stroke, Sid?" Hennessey asked, his gaze never wavering from Margaret's. "I'm a man of many talents. Stroking is only one of them."

Margaret caught her breath.

"When I want something badly enough, like getting this

ball into that hole, I concentrate real hard, making sure I
have everything lined up in the best position to sink it in.''

Hennessey now spoke in a soft, intense voice that Margaret had never heard him use before.

"I don't allow anything to interfere or distract me. Con-
centration is the means to successful completion,'' he said.
"When everything's as ready as I can make it, one smooth
stroke of my shaft does the trick. Trust me on this.'' Hennessey looked meaningfully into Margaret's eyes. "I never
miss the hole.''

Margaret gasped, then covered her trembling mouth with
her equally shaky hand. Why would he do this to her? Why
would he, after all these years, suddenly act as if she was
a woman? A desirable woman?

Hennessey's mouth had formed a firm straight line, and
he clutched the putter tighter. As if he could read her mind,
he said, "We're both going, Mags. Do you understand?''

"I can't.'' She could barely whisper the two words.

Sid turned to her. "I'm ignoring your bad attitude, Margaret. This meeting's over. Give me back my putter,
Johnny. Both of you get in the studio and record 'In Your
Face.' Be at the airport at least an hour before the flight
leaves. Do you understand, Margaret?''

"I'm not going.''

"You'll go, all right. Don't try anything funny. I'm sending that cameraman, you know the one, long hair, holes in
his jeans, glasses—Willie—that's it. He'll be going with
you, watching every move.'' Sid reached inside his top
desk drawer and pulled out an envelope. "Here are the
tickets and itinerary, which you'll follow to the letter. Understand, Margaret? And remember, the reason you're being sent to New York is our little secret.''

Margaret straightened her spine until she stood at her
full, high-heeled height, and glared down at Sid's shiny
bald spot. She would not give him the satisfaction of letting
him know how deeply she despised him at this moment.

After all, she was a St. James, and an expert at masking her emotions, at hiding her fear.

She pivoted, walking regally out of Sid's office and toward her own small cubicle. She left without the golf balls or the tickets. As far as she was concerned, Sid was responsible for killing her. He could take his stupid balls and give them away himself, because there was no way she'd take them with her.

And, like it or not, she'd have to get on that airplane. She'd be a martyr and face death like Joan of Arc. First, though, she had to call Essie and take care of some final business.

No sooner had she sat in her chair, the only piece of furniture in her crowded office not covered with stacks of papers, than the intercom rang and the news director, Chen Ho, told her to get down to the studio, they were waiting for her.

"I'll be there in fifteen minutes," she told him, hanging up on his overdramatic groaning about schedules and rushes.

Margaret had important things to take care of right now. She lifted the receiver and called her mother, catching her on the car phone as Myrna was driving to her father's office to fax the wedding announcement. Myrna didn't take the no-engagement well. "You need to contemplate the direction of your life, dear," her mother had said.

Great. Now Margaret would have to contemplate life, too, along with everything else she had to do. Well, she refused to rush the contemplating part because a person like her shouldn't have to hurry along contemplating her own demise. And her demise is exactly what would happen when she walked on that plane this afternoon.

Margaret pulled a yellow legal pad into her lap, flipped to a blank page, and putting fountain pen to paper, wrote, "To My Loving Sister, Judy Garland St. James: Final Instructions." She lifted the telephone receiver and punched in Essie's number.

While the phone rang in her ear, Margaret wrote on the list: *Tell Essie my will's in the safe-deposit box.*

On the second ring she realized that Essie might have lost the duplicate key to the box. *Second copy of will and another key to box in my underwear drawer. Triple dresser, middle section, top drawer.*

By the third ring she knew she'd have to confess to being the one who had cut off her sister's right braid back in second grade. It would be cruel to let Essie wonder about it the rest of her life. *Tell Essie about hair.* Confession was supposed to be good for the soul and Margaret hoped this confession didn't cost her a grand memorial service after the plane crashed and they recovered her remains.

On the fourth ring she decided as long as she was confessing, she'd call her mother for the second time today, too. She drew a line across the center of the paper, headed it "Mother" and wrote, *Admit that, on final reflection, Mom's idea of me going to medical school to find a director of the board, preferably the chairman, to marry, might not have been such a bad idea, after all.*

Essie finally answered *"Bonjour"* on the fifth ring.

"What took you so long?" Margaret asked. "I've got a whole list of things to discuss with you."

"Tootie, I was just getting ready to call you. Isn't it amazing how our minds are so in tune?" Essie first gushed, then attacked. "How could you have done this without talking to the family first?"

"Done what?"

"You know what you've done. You've—you've—disgraced our family names. All of them. Couldn't you have found someone whose last name was Mitchell? A Margaret Mitchell would have been good. Mother loved *Gone With The Wind.* Although, a Margaret Thatcher would have been okay, too. Everyone loves the Brits. But who ever heard of someone named Margaret Hennessey? Don't you believe in tradition?"

"Forget it. This whole marriage is a hoax. It's Sid's

grand idea to raise the ratings during the November sweeps.'' Margaret told her sister about what had taken place that morning.

"Oh no," Essie moaned. "Do you realize Mother's probably faxed the world your wedding announcement by now?"

"I've already talked to Mom. Luckily, I caught her this morning on her car phone. Anyway, even if she wanted to kill me, which she doesn't, she won't have to because I'm going to New York City."

"You are? How are you getting there?" Essie asked. "By car, bus or train?"

"Flying."

"*You?*"

"Yes, *me.*" Margaret hated to be so sarcastic, but she didn't think Essie had to make it sound as if she was totally spineless. "With Hennessey."

"Oh." After a few moments of silent contemplation, Essie whistled low into the phone. "Oh my, oh my! Are you lucky! Alone, just the two of you, in New York, with that heavenly bod."

"Is that all you can say?"

"Absolutely not, Tootie. Will he give you some?"

"Right. Come on," Margaret denied a little too quickly, grateful her perceptive sister couldn't see her face burning. "As if I'd want any part of him. What do you take me for? Desperate?"

"That's been your problem all along. You just don't know how to have a good time anymore. You never take chances. All of a sudden you got cautious. You, my older sister, my role model who used to sneak out with that guy, Wolfgang, to smoke cigarettes and ride off on his big Harley. Va-room, Va-room."

"That's enough, Essie."

"Okay. Listen, can I ask you something? Promise you won't get mad."

"Go ahead. Ask away. It's not like I have much time on earth left anyway."

"I know when you were the travel reporter at WLS in Chicago, you had a few close calls. I mean, a few elevators that slipped their cables, a few airplanes with frozen wings, a few throws into the rapids. But you're still here. So when did you become afraid of your own shadow?"

"I'm not." Of her shadow at least. "I just got smart. I quit smoking, Harleys, Wolfgang and airplanes." Her fear had no basis in fact. That was the problem with fears. They were irrational, and yet they consumed a person.

Today her life had been taken out of her hands. That didn't make it easier, and it didn't make the vision she'd had of a plane crashing, with her inside, go away. Nor did the sick feeling in the pit of her stomach ease. The thought of putting her life in the hands of people she didn't know, to get her to her destination safely, made her nauseated.

"You're a brave woman, Tootie," Essie said solemnly. "I really admire you."

"Thanks. Well, let's get down to business." Margaret told her sister about the will and safe-deposit box.

"I have a confession to make," Essie said. "I used the duplicate key and went into the box and borrowed your diamond tennis bracelet."

"That's okay." Margaret loved that bracelet, but she wouldn't need it anymore. "You can keep it, my gift. In fact, why don't you go by there today and take the rest of the jewelry, too. Everything I have is yours."

"You mean that?"

"Sure," Margaret said.

"Well, I always really loved your emerald pin. When can I pick it up?"

Margaret clutched the emerald, ruby and diamond brooch pinned right below her left shoulder. Her parents had given it to her as a gift to celebrate the job she'd landed in Chicago at WLS. The pin was designed as a bird in flight. So apropos. "Not on your life, little sister. This baby's going down with me."

"Well, I don't know why you'd want to take it."

"You can use what's left of the pin to identify my charred remains," she said with a snort.

"Oh, that makes sense. You're an all-right sister, always thinking ahead. I miss you already."

"I miss you, too." Okay, so she knew Essie was only placating her, but that's what sisters were for, wasn't it? "I loved being your sister." Margaret's voice caught.

"Well, I have another confession which may make you change your mind. I'd keep it to myself forever, but I don't want you to leave for heaven without knowing."

"You don't?"

"Yep. Remember when I was in third grade, and you had that parakeet, Thomas Jefferson Little Bird Junior Green Pickle Feathers O'Brien St. James?"

"Poor Tommy. You said you found the neighbor's cat in the cage and all that was left were pickled green feathers."

"That's not exactly true. I gave Tommy away to the boy I loved at the time. Remember little Harry Kornacker?"

"That kid who always had the orange Kool-Aid mustache?"

"What can I say? I was in love, and your bird was the only thing in the house that had any value to an eight-year-old boy. He had a bird and he said his bird was lonely."

"Tommy didn't die?" A flood of relief mixed with sisterly hatred ripped through her. She had loved that bird.

"Not only didn't he die, but Harry changed Tommy's name to Tammy and she had cute little green baby birds."

Moments before Essie's confession, Margaret had decided not to tell her about the braid. In fact, she'd even scratched it off the list. But giving away Tommy, even though it was twenty years ago, changed everything. "I suppose I should make my confession before I head to the big space in the sky," Margaret said.

"Sure, go ahead."

"I'm the one who cut your braid. While you were sleeping. I couldn't stand your snoring, and thought if your head was a little lighter, you'd stop. So snip, snip went one-half of all that beautiful hair you had, sliced right off. Down the middle. If you still want it back, it's in a plastic bag in the attic, labeled Dirty Diapers."

"I knew that, Tootie-Hootie. You silly thing. Why do you think I gave Harry the bird?"

Why, that stinker! Baby sisters weren't supposed to get back at their big sisters. Big sisters were the bosses. They should be able to do all kinds of stupid things and get away with them. Wasn't there an unwritten sister law or something that said that?

Essie sweetly said, "You remember the pink sweater you loved? The one with the white fur collar? Well, those weren't moth holes, you know. I used a hole puncher."

"You little creep."

"I know."

For the first time all day, Margaret really smiled. "I've got news for you, shrimp face. I'm the one who put honey in your sheets at camp."

"Oh yeah, well, I'm the one who put the fly in your soda at Christmas dinner when you were ten."

"What you didn't know was I found it and stuck it inside your hamburger, which *you ate*."

Margaret leaned back and relaxed. "Oh, you think you were so smart. Well, I'm the one who..."

4

"HEY, HO!" John called out to the news director as he followed Mags into the studio.

"Don't 'Hey, Ho' me." Chen Ho stopped pacing in front of the anchor set and descended on them. "You're a traitor to single guys everywhere. But to me most of all. Your *amigo.* Your *compadre.*"

"Poor, poor Chen." Mags waved a fluttering dismissive hand in the air. "Has to find another role model. What's a man to do?"

"And you, Margaret." The news director turned his anger toward her. "I used to respect you. How can you marry this guy?" Chen stuck his thumb in John's chest. "You don't even like him."

"I like him." Mags grimaced.

What a jerk he'd been just fifteen minutes ago, feeling sorry for her. Her, Miss High-and-Mighty, whose expression couldn't hide just how she felt about marriage to him, even a fake marriage.

John turned away. There was nothing he could do about the situation now. But he could try and pacify Chen. "I know you're mad now, but believe me when I tell you everything'll work out."

"Believe you? What a joke." Chen, normally mild-mannered, exploded. "We've passed ABC and NBC in the 6:00 p.m. time slot. We've got the best chance we've ever had at overtaking CBS for first place. Then what happens? You two, sworn enemies, decide to marry. Gimme a break here. Right now we're sucking the wind from the Houston markets. When this wedding takes place, we'll just suck. End of story. End of first place. End of six o'clock news.''

"I sense a little hostility here." John could work around that.

"I hear you two are taking off to New York on a pre-honeymoon? Why don't you just rent a room right here at the Marriott if you're so hot to trot—which, by the way, I know you're not.''

"It's strictly platonic, Chen. No hanky-panky. Anyway, Willie will be there and he'll be overnighting tape. The ratings won't suffer. If anything, they'll pick up.''

"Here's a newsflash for you. The ratings may be great up to the day of the wedding. But the morning after, you'll hit bottom. You can kiss my profits—and yours—good-bye.''

John had spent his whole broadcasting career being patient, waiting for someone to notice him, waiting for someone to overlook his lack of education, waiting for the big break to come. Now he had the opportunity and he wasn't going to pass it up. Someone else was going to have to step aside for him this time. He'd stepped aside often enough for everyone else. In a voice of stone, he told the director, "It's out of my hands.''

"What about our stock in this hole-in-the-wall place? Huh? Did you think of that, smart guy?''

Taking the pygmy salary package offered by Rachel seemed like a small sacrifice to get a break in the TV business. At the time he thought he was the only one on the payroll getting minimum wage and worthless KSLT stock. Employees talked, though, and he now knew everyone who worked here got the same package, including Mags.

John could sympathize with Chen's anger, to a point. Over the last year, under Rachel's financial expertise, their KSLT stock had started paying pretty good dividends. Still... "Come on, Chen. You're looking at the short term.''

"Wrong. I'm looking at the long term. Once you're mar-

ried, no one's going to watch this newscast. It's the anticipation of the sex you and Margaret *don't* have that turns
the public on. Marriage kills sexual attraction.''

"I wouldn't know, would I?" John took his place next
to Mags who'd developed a bad case of rigor mortis since
he'd seen her minutes before. She stared, glassy-eyed, into
the ozone layer of the studio. Her shoulders and back were
straight and rigid, her long, slender fingers tented on top of
the "In Your Face" script.

The proof of her comatose state of mind was in her but-
tons.

Two little pearly ones were undone, allowing the white
blouse to gape open over her breasts. Breasts as luscious-
looking as he'd remembered. That little flesh-colored lacy
thing she had poured herself into was a wet dream waiting
to happen.

"Why, my little Mag-o-muffin," he growled softly.
"You seem to be partially undone." He skimmed the silky
material of her blouse, resisting the urge to delve farther,
to feel the soft, plump skin.

Margaret felt Hennessey's fingers touching her clothes,
looked down and twisted out of his reach. She didn't have
the energy to come at him with her usual witty repartee.
The retorts he found so amusingly insulting. She had to
concentrate now on doing two things at once—rebuttoning
her blouse and learning how to breathe again.

She heard Chen's voice through her earphone, "Margaret, get ready. Five, four, three, two, one, go."

She surrounded herself with what little composure she
had left, which wasn't much, and smiled serenely into their
only camera when the tally light came on. And smiling was
the last thing Margaret felt like doing. She hadn't been able
to make Sid understand just how devastating her fear of
flying was, how even the thought of getting on an airplane
all but paralyzed her.

"Margaret," Chen said louder. "Dead air is a bad
thing."

So was a dead Margaret.

"Margaret!" Chen yelled. "Your damn commentary!"

What was Chen's problem? She cleared her throat. "Several days ago, some gormless person sneaked onto the front lawn of the courthouse in the middle of the night and poisoned the one-hundred-year-old live oak tree that has been gracing our halls of justice. This copycat version of the Treaty Oak poisoning that took place in Austin several years ago is, in my not so humble opinion, an act of treason against the people of Sugar Land.

"Now the fate of our tree is in the hands of city council." *Just like my life will be in the hands of some airplane mechanic who could very well have forgotten to screw on the lug nuts, if there were even lug nuts to screw on an airplane.*

"They want to chop down the tree," she went on. "Citizens of Sugar Land, what about our lovely birds who live in the tree? 'Where's my nest?' they'll chirp, flying around in the sky, disoriented. They'll tangle up in each other's wings, like, to give an example, airplanes in our overcrowded, rush-hour airspace. How many midair collisions will be on your, the public's, conscience? How many fragile wings will break apart, sending bodies dive-bombing to earth and crash-landing on the pavement with giant-size splats?"

Margaret stopped to take a few deep breaths.

The studio was quiet. Too quiet. Hennessey's Adam's apple bobbed. His own typewritten, fifteen-second script rustled in the tight grip of his fingers.

"Mags, this is a tree commentary. Remember? It's not about birds." He pointed to the wrinkled papers crumpled in her hand. "You're not reading from your script."

"Listen, Hennessey, I'm ad-libbing. Do you think you have a corner on the ad-libbing market? I can ad-lib if I want."

"Okay, ad-lib. Geez." He stared at her.

Let him stare if that's what made him happy. Fine. They

might not like each other, still, they'd been sitting next to each other for almost three years now, and had gotten to know each other well enough to *know* they didn't like each other.

They were the very best of adversaries. Someone as close to her as Hennessey should have acted like a true Southern gentleman and refused to go to New York, the trip of death.

A man who not thirty minutes ago had claimed to be a sensitive man was acting, on purpose, like just a plain ol' everyday man man.

She ignored Chen's switch to Chinese in her earphones, and pleaded to the camera, "Don't let some silver missile of death take your friends away. Save us."

John looked over at the normally sophisticated, articulate St. James woman next to him. She had turned into a lunatic. "Silver missile?" He ripped his script in half. "Save us?"

Chen, finally going back to English, yelled, "Cut. Cut-cut-cut. Cut."

The Magpie had finally flown the coop. She gave Chen a serene look, and said, "I'm finished now anyway."

"I wish I'd been prepared." John took both halves of his script and ripped the paper into fourths, then eighths. He kept tearing until the papers were in minuscule pieces. "Next time, Magpie, give a guy some warning when you decide to ad-lib." He threw the confetti into the air and let them flutter down. "Look at them flying—and falling. Just like little magpies."

She gasped.

John looked over at her, and for once she looked back at him, too. Her cornflower-blue eyes were large and fearful.

Damn. She was getting to him. He felt it in his gut, the twisting kind of sick feeling when a guy knew he should do something heroic to help the lady out. Maybe he should march into Sid's office and tell the little man that he refused to go on the trip. Then Mags could stay home in her safe little world, continue to make his life miserable with her higher-than-mighty attitude, and he'd be right here at KSLT, where he had no prospects for any sort of future.

He wasn't going to do it. He couldn't help her. Not this time. Hell. Millions of people were afraid to fly, and they flew anyway. Mags would get over it once they were in the air.

She unpinned her mike, laid it on the desk, and said, "I know you want to be the next Peter Jennings and you think this New York trip is the only chance you'll ever get. But you have to understand something. I can't go with you. You'll have to go alone."

"Don't you think I wish I could? Don't you think I'd like not having to worry that I might meet someone interested in offering me a screen test and you'll walk in the room."

"What difference does that make?" Her blue eyes widened, her black lashes clumped together with moisture.

"Because then I become a nobody, because you're always the somebody. That's what *always* happens. You saw a sample of it in Sid's office. Cuddle Me Clothing and Fabulous Fat-Free Foods want to meet *us*. Not me, not you, us. Weren't you listening? We're a package deal. It's happened this way every time."

"That's not true."

"Oh, babe, you don't even have a clue, do you? You're prime rib, and I'm the horseradish sauce on the side. They'll take the prime rib with or without the sauce, but they'll never take the sauce without the prime rib."

"Oh, Hennessey." Her tone denied his words.

"How do you think I feel? Every station wants to hire the elusive Margaret St. James, newscaster, Rice grad-u-ate, and award-winning reporter. The modern-day Greta Garbo. You're offered jobs all over, all the time. No one's willing to take a chance on me, unless you're part of the package."

"I've never been offered the job in Houston that I want. If one of the Houston stations had an opening and wanted me, I'd leave here and you'd never have to worry about getting stuck with me again.''

''Am I supposed to feel sorry for you because the one job you want hasn't come through? Give me a break. If you haven't been offered a job in Houston, then that's the only job in this country you haven't been offered.''

''I'm just trying to tell you that I have no intention of leaving this area. My family is here. We don't always get what we want. Not me. Not you.''

''Remember that. Because you want to stay here, and I want to go to New York. And we're going.''

''I'm sorry,'' she said softly, shaking her head.

''Prove it,'' he demanded. ''Get on that plane with me.''

Neither spoke for several long minutes. Finally, she pushed herself off the chair and without looking behind her, her head held high, she walked from the studio.

''Mags!'' he called out as she neared the door. ''Will you be at the airport?''

The studio door banging shut was his answer.

''Don't do this to me, Mags,'' he yelled into the empty studio.

John pushed the hundreds of tiny scraps of paper, all that were left of his never-used script, off the desk. Taking a deep, ragged breath, he stared at the door Mags had just slammed shut on his future and pounded his fist on the desk so hard a half-full cup of coffee spilled over. ''Damn. Dammit to hell.''

JOHN PACED the distance between the dozen or so glass doors outside Terminal C at Houston's Bush Intercontinental Airport. He'd already lost track of how many times he'd looked at his watch, how many times he'd gone over to the curb so he could inspect the people getting out of the steady stream of cars, buses and taxis pulling up to the terminal. Hundreds of passengers were dropped off, but nowhere in the crowd did he spot Mags's familiar blond head.

Only forty-five minutes until takeoff and he knew in his gut she wouldn't show up.

He talked himself into believing that Mags not tagging along to New York would be a good thing. He wouldn't have to defend his years of broadcast experience—which he'd slightly exaggerated…okay, lied through his teeth about when he'd applied to KSLT for the sportscaster job. Sid had never checked his references, and John had done his job well.

His talent was the one thing he'd never had to lie about. His talent had gotten him promoted to coanchor of the 6:00 p.m. and 11:00 p.m. news—not any golf game, no matter what the Magpie wanted to think.

New York. Nothing would hold him back now. For the first time, right within his grasp, was the opportunity to reach for that elusive star.

John Patrick Hennessey was going places without Margaret St. James there to entice network news directors, hypnotize them, make them believe, whether intentionally or not, that without her the team would sink. If Mags wasn't around on this trip, he'd finally get the chance to prove he could do the job on his own. He had experience—maybe not the ten years they wanted, but still, he had the ratings to offset the experience. That was the key to success. Not having a college degree. Not having a real high-school diploma.

John had made a promise to himself a long time ago and he'd kept it. He regularly visited Sugar Land high schools and talked to troubled kids, convincing them not to drop out the way he'd done. Sure, he'd earned a GED, but he knew he'd have been more successful if he'd stayed in school. He never should have quit.

Quit. That word and "Mags" didn't belong in the same sentence either.

John paced faster. Maybe she'd gotten into a car accident. Maybe she'd gone to Hobby Airport, instead of Bush. Maybe she'd gotten lost. Maybe she was sick. That bird, tree, exploding, dive-bombing, "In Your Face" commentary she'd done this morning could have been a sign that she'd finally cracked. Maybe falling apart was something normal that happened to blue bloods like her. Maybe he shouldn't have pushed her so hard at the end. But how was he supposed to know that Mags would go over the top?

John walked back to the curb and watched more people unload from vehicles. A chauffeur opened the back door of a black stretch and held out his hand. John immediately recognized the trim ankle, the shapely curved calf, rounded knee and slender thigh. He'd recognize those Tina Turner legs anywhere. A heavy jolt of adrenaline shot through his veins, whether from disappointment that Mags had come, or anticipation of the next four days, he couldn't say.

But a limo? How did she rate a limousine when he had to drive himself and park in a public parking lot? Then he remembered. She was a St. James.

He took the five steps over to where she still sat, half in, half out of the stretch. "Well?" He raised an eyebrow, his lips twisted into a tight smile.

"What?" she snapped, peeking out of the car, glaring up at his face.

"Wasn't sure you'd make it."

"Of course I'd make it."

"Then what the hell took you so long? You were supposed to be here an hour ago."

With the chauffeur's help, Mags stepped, like a queen, from the limousine and landed so close to John's chest the tips of her breasts grazed his shirt. He steeled himself against the sudden heat that the whisper of a touch had caused to blaze through his veins.

She wore a sweet, innocent smile. "The plane doesn't leave for—" she glanced at her watch "—at least forty minutes."

He knew that smile. In fact, he'd had an intimate relationship with that smile, and didn't like it one bit.

The chauffeur tipped his cap and got back in the limo.

"Wait a second," John yelled out to him. "You forgot the baggage."

"She's it." The limo pulled away from the curb, leaving only Mags behind.

John slowly turned to face her. He knew, even though she watched him with her guileless ocean eyes, she was plotting ways to make his life as miserable as she was feeling right now.

He wouldn't let her. "Where are they?"

"Who?" She sniffed daintily and stuck her aristocratic nose in the air.

"Not who. They. Your suitcases. Those square boxes that carry clothes, makeup, underwear." He grabbed her arm. "Do you understand what I'm saying? I don't share toothbrushes."

"I understand exactly what you're saying." She shrugged out of his grasp. Her cheeks had turned pink and her breathing came faster. "*I'm* not stupid."

He refused to be baited. "You're not going to screw up this trip for me, Mag-o-muffin."

"Believe me, I have no intention of screwing—anything that has to do with you."

"Mar-ga-ret."

"You mean you really know how to pronounce my name? I know it's got a lot of letters, but I've been telling you all along it's only three syllables."

He took a long, deep breath—and coughed out exhaust fumes.

A frown creased between those carefully shaped eyebrows of hers and her eyes and mouth softened. What could that mean? Concern? Sympathy? For him? Not likely.

"All right," she said grudgingly. "Fine. Here's my luggage." She held up her purse. "You win. You always win."

"What're you talking about?"

"Look." She snapped it open, taking out a gold credit

card, waving it in front of his face. "All I need is right here. *If* we get to New York—"

"If? We're getting to New York and there's nothing you're going to do to stop us, do you understand?"

"Like I said, *if* we get to New York, I'll go shopping for whatever I need there."

She wanted to go shopping? In New York? On his time? On his future?

"Why are you looking at me so funny? I know they have stores in New York, so what's your problem?"

"You. You're my problem. Let's go." He took her by the hand and pulled her behind him through the electronic doors.

"So tell me, how's Willie?" Mags asked, sounding breathless. "Did he and the camera make it here okay?"

"Willie's fine. His camera's fine. His mother in Galveston is fine."

He took longer steps, she breathed harder. Served her right for driving him insane. And he didn't even have blue blood or a pedigree for an excuse.

"Stop a minute, will you?" She tried to pull him backward. "I need to fix my shoe."

John glanced down at her black pumps and grunted, "Not on your life, baby doll." He kept pulling her, not slowing down until they reached the metal security detectors. "Shove your *suitcase* onto the belt."

She hesitated, gnawing at her lip.

"Now!" he barked.

Her lower lip started to tremble, which made him go hard, which ticked him off royally. He dug his nails into his palms to keep from doing something drastic. Like pulling her into his arms. He was a sick man. "Do it!"

"I know what to do." She tossed her purse onto the black conveyor belt, then stood just north of the arched steel canopy leading into the terminals.

Through gritted teeth, John told her, "As much as I love the view of your cute little cupcakes, Mag-o-muffin—"

She whipped her head around. "Stop punning my name. I'm sick of it."

"—I'd like your buns a lot better over there." He gave her a gentle shove, pushing her through the metal detector. She's sick of it? What a joke. He'd make sure the seat assignments had him in the bulkhead and her in the toilet, where her shaky lips couldn't get him in trouble.

She took the purse off the conveyor belt and stood still, clutching it to her breasts, crushing everything, waiting.

Waiting? For him? "Listen, Mags, you and me, we're supposed to be lovers, not fighters," he reasoned with her.

He waited a second, but when she didn't come back with any "I'll never be a lover to you," he got more than a little worried, especially when she placed her hand in his and walked quietly beside him.

Now what was going on? He leaned down, taking in the spicy-sweet perfume she wore. He liked her scent.

He didn't want to like the way she smelled. He didn't want to like anything about her. He especially didn't want to like the way her small, soft hand felt inside his own. He didn't want to wonder why she'd given him her hand at all.

He had to snap out of these kinds of wimpy thoughts and harden his heart. If he didn't, he'd only get hurt in the end.

They had almost reached the gate when she jerked herself to a stop, stomped her foot, and said, "I want to go home." She had his hand twisted behind him since he refused either to let her go, or stop for her. "Now," she snapped.

He could see Willie slouching against a pillar near the check-in counter, his eyes closed. KSLT's only remote camera, a secondhand RCA camcorder Sid bought in a pawnshop before John had started working at the station, and some carry-on bags were behind Willie, out of the cameraman's sight, including John's duffel bag. Great watchdog, that Willie.

"Four days," John said. "That's all I'm asking for."

"There won't be four days, there won't be any days," Mags predicted. "Just go yourself. And if you actually make it to New York alive, you can tell Sid I went. He'll never know the difference."

"Wouldn't I like to," John said through clenched teeth. "Only we've got a spy with a camera, who'll get pictures back to Sugar Land in no time, showing Sid exactly where you aren't."

"Maybe I can bribe Willie. He looks like he could be had, cheap."

"Stop acting like a spoiled rich kid." John looked down at her at the same moment she looked up at him. What was she trying to tell him with those big eyes of hers? He had called her spoiled. Fighting words. Where was the fight? Where was her spirit?

"Toooootttt-eeeeee."

Any color left in Mags's already-pale face completely drained. Her eyes widened and her lips parted in a perfect Cupid's bow. Even Willie woke up from his nap, looking around dazed.

"Tootie, Tootie, Tootie." The chorus of voices came closer.

He spotted them halfway down the terminal. Four women, all blond, but stepping stones apart in age, moved toward them.

"Uh-oh," Mags said under her breath. "I don't believe this. Hurry up. Hide me."

"Not on your life, babe." Whoever they were, this should be good.

"Tootie!"

"Do you know those women?" he asked.

"Don't ask."

"T-o-o-o-otie!"

"What's a tootie?"

"I told you not to ask," Mags hissed through her smile. After three years, he had gotten to know Mags and her smiles pretty well. As far as smiles went, this one looked sick.

"Mother!" Mags threw open her arms and a tall slender woman embraced her, blowing kisses past each cheek.

"Grandma Lillie." Mags disentangled herself from the mom and leaned down over the oldest woman, kissing her paper-thin cheek.

"Grandma Clara." She gave the other elderly woman a kiss and hug. "Essie, what a surprise." Mags grimaced at the youngest of the four. "I bet this was all your idea."

"Wanted to get one last look at the brooch. Nice." Essie didn't seem fazed by Mags's expression. If anything, her grin blossomed.

Mags's fingers immediately wrapped protectively around the emerald pin. "Why are you all here?"

"We're family, darling. We had to come to the airport and wish you a bon voyage." Essie's arms were covered with diamond and gold bracelets, her ears with emerald earrings, and hanging from her neck were beads of gold, silver and many other brilliant colors. "Wanted to make sure you saw everything." She jangled her arms. "And everyone you'd miss while you're away." Essie's laughter sparkled brighter than the jewels covering her body.

The more miserable Mags looked, the more John enjoyed the show. He'd never really thought of Mags actually having a family, except in the most abstract kind of way. Who would have thought they were real people? For some reason, John had assumed she'd been birthed in outer space and sent here for the sole purpose of making his life on earth hell. Finding out she had relatives was like the time in third grade when he saw his teacher and her husband and kids at the local restaurant one Sunday morning. He realized then that teachers ate like real people.

"Tootie, darling, we couldn't let you go without saying goodbye," the mother said, then turned toward John. "And seeing who your traveling companion was."

"Oh, Mother, you know Mr. Hennessey." Essie's eyelids dipped coyly. "You drool over him every night, along with the rest of us."

"Thanks." John nodded slightly.

Essie turned to her sister. "We had to wish you well, Toots, a soft takeoff, and landing, and all that other good stuff."

John looked down on the top of Mags's golden head. "Are you a Tootie?"

She ignored him. He smirked. So typically rich. Only the elite could afford to have stupid nicknames like Skip and Scooter and Muffin and Tootie. So Mags is really a Tootie, whatever that was. In his circle, nicknames ranged from Dogbreath and Snotnose, to Big Mama and Hips. In his neighborhood, any guy named Skip would be treated to a nose job, courtesy of Dogbreath.

John put his arm around Mags's stiff shoulders and drew her close to his side, giving her a little squeeze. It felt like squeezing cardboard. "Aren't you going to introduce me to these beautiful women, my sweet little Magpie?"

He thought about calling her Tootie, but the sudden vision of Mags tooting his horn made him go hot. And hard. More than what her shaking lip did to him. His hand tightened around her shoulder. He needed release from all the tension surrounding this woman.

"How could I have forgotten my manners?" The way she said it made him think she'd like nothing better than to forget.

"John Hennessey, this is my mother, Myrna Loy St. James, my great-grandma, Lillian Gish, and my grandmother, Clara Bow Mann."

"Aren't you forgetting someone, my little Magpie?" John asked.

"My sister, Judy Garland St. James. We call her Essie. This is John Hennessey. Oh, I already said that. Well, you know..."

"Oh, we know only too well, don't we, Mother?" Essie

ran her gaze up and down John's body like a paintbrush,
trying to figure out where she should start stroking.

He wanted to say to the younger duplicate of his Magpie,
"Tsk, tsk, little sister, it's not nice to move in on big sister's territory." Even if he really wasn't. Her territory.

"A magpie?" Great-grandmother Lillian asked. Her loud
voice clashed with her frail-looking body. "Isn't that some
kind of bird? Who would call our Tootie a bird?"

"Did you call our Tootie a bird, Mr. Hennessey?"
Myrna's pleasant smile didn't quite reach her eyes.

"Only with the deepest affection and love." John lowered his lips until he reached Mags's temple. The rapid
throbbing of her pulse underneath his mouth made his own
pulse jump. He planted a sloppy kiss with a loud smack,
and gave her stiff shoulder another squeeze. Her heel
plowed down on the top of his foot. The same foot she'd
gotten earlier today. His old Mags had come alive, and she
was wicked.

"Oh, look. We're going to be on TV." Essie dimpled
for Willie, who had found the camera. He zoomed onto the
young woman's face, then scanned the rest of Mags's family, documenting the St. James bon voyage party.

John whispered in Mags's ear, "You'll have to tell me
why your family are all named after dead movie stars."

"They're not all dead." Then she turned away, ignoring
him.

Good, he thought. More ammunition for New York if
she tried anything sneaky. Tootie. He liked it.

Great-grandma Lillian perked up for the camera. "Are
we going to be in the movies?" She whacked her daughter
Clara on the arm. "You see, I told you I did the right thing
naming you Clara Bow. Now look in the camera and dimple."

The final-boarding announcement came over the loudspeaker. John grinned indulgently at the St. James women,
but didn't take his hold off of Mags, figuring she'd bolt if
given the chance. "We've got to check in."

The group surrounded the couple, escorting them to the counter. He liked her family, and they seemed to accept him, which was not what he had expected from them at all.

"Are you really going to get my Tootie to go on that airplane?" Myrna asked. "With all those people?"

Maybe he'd been wrong—maybe the most important member, the mother, didn't accept him at all. John recognized Myrna's pert nose in the air as an exact duplicate of her daughter's. Just as he recognized the accusing tone of her voice, as if he was supposed to charter a plane to take the aristocrat, Miss Tootie, to New York City. "I know it's not the Concorde, Mrs. St. James, or a private jet." John hated sounding defensive. He took a deep breath. He wasn't horse manure. He was a man. A good man. His voice was deep and sure. "We'll get to New York safely and I promise I'll take care of your daughter. Nothing will happen to her."

"We're all counting on that, dear," Myrna said soothingly. "And I say that any man who can get her on that plane deserves a medal."

"Thanks." He hadn't counted on that reaction. John handed their tickets to the woman behind the counter and waited while she checked the computer, then gave him the boarding passes.

"Now I know you and my little Tootie are getting married in name only. She told me all about that."

"She did?" He wanted to know just how much more Mags had spilled.

"Of course she did." Myrna patted his arm and gushed. "But you know, and I know, that even when it's 'in name only,' things happen."

"Things won't happen."

"I'm sure they won't, dear. But if they do, please don't hurt her. And be sure to use a condom."

"Mrs. St. James—"

"Mother!" Mags woke up.

"Yes!" Essie exclaimed. "Tootie's alive."

John stared at Myrna. She'd just given him permission to marry her daughter, and not in name only. But completely. She'd accepted him. Him. John P. Hennessey.

That was great, but "in name only" was what he wanted. He wasn't ready for marriage. Not him.

"So," Myrna continued. "When you have children, there will be no Brad Pitts. Our family has females. It's a tradition."

"That's not true," Clara cut in. "Remember your cousin Carole Lombard Harrison had those twins. One she named Sonny Bono, and the other Cher."

"Oh, Mother, please. Those were rock-star names," Myrna argued.

"Sonny was still a boy child," Clara grumbled. "Which was my point. If he—" she pointed at John "—wants to have a boy, and name him a pit, he can do it."

"All right, Mother."

"The plane's already been boarded, Mr. Hennessey, Ms. St. James," the lady behind the counter said. "You'd better hurry. I'll call the crew and tell them you're on your way. Don't worry, they won't leave without you. And by the way, I love your news shows. I watch both of them every night."

Willie and the camera were at the departure gate leading to the airplane, the film rolling, the red light on the camera flashing.

John handed the boarding passes to the gate attendant and waited as she tore the seating cards in half and handed the other half back to him. He faced Mags. "Let's get this show going, Magpie."

"I *can* do this," she mumbled, her spine straight, her legs moving in a forward motion. Even if her blue eyes had glazed over like fog over the sea.

"It was nice meeting all of you." John waved to Mags's family.

"Yes, dear, it certainly was, wasn't it?" Myrna said.

"He's better-looking in person than on TV," Lillian offered.

Clara Bow pinched his rear. "Good muscles. Like a young Doug Fairbanks. Hubba hubba!"

Essie looked into her sister's face, and said, "You'll be all right. I never worry about flying, 'cause I'm such a bad driver. I figure a plane has got to be safer than a car with me at the wheel."

"I'm a good driver," Mags said. "I've never been in an accident. This will be my very first—and only—crash."

"Ah, honey, I'm telling you, the plane won't crash. You'll be fine."

"Is there a problem?" John asked.

Four golden-haired women came together in perfect unison, and shook their heads.

The fifth, Mags, nodded her head at the same time, declaring, "No problem."

John looked at her and shrugged. "Okay, let's get going. We'll send postcards," he promised the other women.

"That'll be great," Essie said.

"I'd like one of a naked statue."

That must have been from Clara.

Willie, ahead of them, walked backward, tripping on the irregularities in the walkway and his untied shoelaces, keeping the camera focused on them.

John, with Mags walking stonily beside him, got as far as the open hatch when she stopped moving. The flight attendants inside the plane beckoned them to hurry on board. The pilots' cockpit door was open.

"Mags?" he asked softly. "Can you walk?"

"Sure I can," she said so softly he had to strain to hear her words. "But here's the thing, Hennessey." Her voice cracked in between the syllables. "I think this has to do with control. In an airplane I don't have any. If I knew how to fly a plane, then I'd know if the pilots were doing it right."

"You're scared."

"No. Not that."

"Mags, come on. Everyone's a little afraid. If they say they're not, they're lying."

"Okay, I'm scared."

"We can work through that."

"But there's more. Five years ago, I had a vision. It all came back to me the moment Sid said we were taking an airplane. I saw a giant, long, silver missile engulfed in flames, crashing to earth," she said intensely.

He gently placed his arm around her waist. "Magpie."

"If I get on that plane," she whispered, "it's going to crash."

"It's not going to crash." He brushed a strand of blond hair off her cheek, gently tucking it behind her small ear. "I'll be here with you. I won't let anything happen to you. I promise you'll be okay."

Then the blue-blooded, practical Mags did something he'd never expected.

She burst into tears.

5

A FEW MINUTES and half a box of tissues later, Mags had finally calmed down enough, much to John's relief, to board the plane. He'd never seen her like this. And he didn't know how to deal with this new, uncontrolled person.

"I'mokay," Mags mumbled. "Iwisheveryonewouldleavemealone."

"What did she say?" Linda the flight attendant asked.

Since John had a long and intimate association with Mags and her mumbling, he interpreted, "Mags is telling you thank you very much for caring about her. She's going to be fine."

"I'mgoingtomakeit. Hennesseygoawayanddie."

"She said she's going to make it, and that you shouldn't worry, she appreciates all you've done. And she's dying to take off."

"GetlostIhateyourguts."

"Now she's saying you shouldn't waste any more time on her because she's going to prove she's brave and conquer her fear. She has guts."

"Oh," Linda cooed. "Isn't she admirable." She smiled, obviously thinking the crisis was over and went back to her work.

Right. Admirable. What wasn't admirable was how much he liked the way Mags's soft, delicate hand, firmly bound to his own, felt as if it belonged there permanently. He wasn't in the market for anyone permanently.

He'd always liked Mags, even when she was being her

hoity-toity self. He also knew that if the normally strong, independent, never-needing-anybody Mags was fully conscious, she'd never let him hold on to her the way he was right now, with their fingers intertwined, palm skimming palm, wrist rubbing wrist.

Maybe it was nothing, just an aftermath from meeting her family. Or that for the first time since the night he walked out of her house, the wall she'd built around herself started to crack. He had to admit, he kind of liked this new, submissive Magpie.

He also knew that at any time, the old Mags could come back, and whether her family accepted him or not, he'd once again be from the wrong side of the tracks.

Mags stalled next in front of the divider separating first-class from coach.

"Never been past first-class before?" John tugged her arm gently.

"Of course I have." Her voice wasn't much more than a mutter. "I can do this. I can fly. Look at the space shuttle."

"That's right, Mags. Think rocket ships. So let's go. One foot in front of the other," he coaxed gently. "Good girl. You're doing fine. This is what's called walking. Remember?" At the rate they were moving—somewhere around an inch an hour—they should make their seats, oh, in three days.

Pulling her along wasn't easy. He'd lifted weights since he was twelve, had run eight miles a day for the past three years, and still, even with all his strength, he couldn't get her to move any faster. He didn't know how she'd managed to do it, but when he wasn't looking she must have poured concrete in her panty hose.

"The pilot can't take off until we're in our seats," he said, realizing too late that was definitely the wrong information to hand over.

Meanwhile, Willie's camcorder was recording every painful step.

"You'll have to set the film at fast-forward for the news," John called to the cameraman.

"Huh?" Willie asked.

Great. Willie's already sleepwalking. "Come on, Magpie. We've got to move. You're not being cute."

"What's wrong with your eyes, sonny?" the elderly man they had stopped next to asked. "This here girl's a looker." His dentures clacked together. "Sit in my lap, girlie-girl?" Shaggy white eyebrows did the Groucho dance.

John twisted around, willing Mags to look into his eyes, to see how their situation had gotten urgent. Linda was latching overhead compartments behind them.

"I'm coming, Hennessey. I'm taking this slow, absorbing each and every moment remaining in my life." She had a serene smile on her lips and her blue eyes seemed to be at peace.

When she started to hum "The Battle Hymn of the Republic," *My eyes have seen the glory of the coming of the Lord,* he took that as a sign things were going to be just fine.

John grinned as people sitting near where they stood waved pens, pencils and in-flight magazines in his direction. "Autograph, Mr. Hennessey." "Can you sign right here, Johnny?" "I love you, John! Don't marry her, marry me."

John autographed and smiled his professional smile for everyone. After all, these were the people who had brought their newscast to number two and would soon make it number one. "Thank you, everyone. Thank you," he said, then saw that Mags had taken a step backward. "Mags!"

He tugged her hand harder. "I can't believe you'd leave this plane just because my fan club seems to be here, and yours isn't."

"Oh, please," she said haughtily. "Real broadcasters don't have fan clubs." Then she stopped. "I need to stay right here and contemplate the fact that you do."

No way, he thought, was she going to get away with

that. If there'd been room, and if he could do it without knocking an innocent passenger in the face with her feet, he would've just hauled off, swung Mags up over his shoulder and carried her down the aisle of the plane.

"Let's do the contemplating when we get to our seats."

"Okay, as long as you remember my need to contemplate."

"I'll remember, all right."

She moved forward again.

The circulating-air system let loose with a vaporized film from the upper vents, misting the windows. The buzz from the air conditioner clicked on and off. Out of the corner of his eye, John saw more pens and paper being thrust toward him, only this time he ignored them.

A buxom brunette flounced into the aisle in front of him, blocking their path and stopping their progress. She held up a blue pen, and breathed out heavily, "Will you autograph me, Johnny, darlin'?"

The woman pointed the pen's tip in the direction of her breasts. John wasn't even tempted, but years of public relations kicked in. With a tight smile, he said, "Sure, honey. Later."

She tapped her chest with the pen. "You betcha."

"Mr. Hennessey, I'll have to ask you to take your seat now. You, too, Ms. St. James," Linda said, holding a yellow oxygen mask dangling from a piece of elastic off her finger. "We can't take off until you're seated."

John's head snapped around. "In a second."

She backed away, her head dipping coyly. "Take two."

"We're almost there, Magpie," John said. "Only sixteen more steps." He tugged, she moved, and they continued that way, not stopping until they reached their seats. "These are great. Right over the wings. Wings are good things."

No response from her. Maybe when Mags started contemplating, she went into a trance. He could use this to his advantage if he gave her enough material to contemplate.

Willie, with his long hair coming out of the ponytail, straddled the center seat in the row ahead of them, the camera hanging over the seat back, the lens aimed in Mags's direction. John guided her into the row, and ordered, "Sit." When she didn't respond, he placed both hands on her shoulders and pushed.

Down she went, staring straight ahead, nose to camera lens.

"Hey, man, they made me go to my seat, so I missed some of you and Margaret walking through the cabin." The cameraman's slow, sleepy voice dragged over them. "What took you so long?"

"Mags is contemplating," John said.

"C-o-o-o-o-l." Willie pulled the camera back a little and tinkered with the lens before shoving it back in her face. "So tell the people back home what you two lovebirds will be *contemplating* on doing in New York City?"

"Who died and made you reporter?" John asked, keeping his hand firmly on Mags's left knee in case she got a burst of energy and decided to make one last escape attempt.

"Well, you ain't doing much talking," Willie grumbled. "Come on, Mags, hurry up, Mags," he mimicked. "Got a story to film, news at six and eleven, central standard time."

"Since the film is going back on an overnight carrier, there won't be any story until tomorrow. Take a break, will you."

Mags grasped his arm and, using her on-air anchor voice, said, "I'm happy to be here. I knew once I walked on this jet I would be fine. I feel just glorious inside. The fear of flying has burst out of my body. Are you with me on this?"

"At your side." He nodded.

"Fear of flying is stupid, right?"

He looked at her skeptically. "Right."

John continued looking at her, long and hard. Large pools of blue eyes too big for her face. High aristocratic cheekbones. Full, pink lips, slightly parted over orthodontically perfect straight teeth. Golden hair, straight to her shoulders. Elegant. Regal. He was drawn to her eyes again. Fear.

This was going to be one long ride.

Another flight attendant, Wanda, asked them to fasten their seat belts. When Mags made no move, John reached over to help her. "Magpie, you're sitting on the belt." No response. "Mags?" Nothing. He had no choice. Not really. She needed *him*. Not just to get the ratings up, but on a deeper, more emotional level. To help her get her belt on. He gently slipped his hand under her thigh, feeling for the wayward strap, doing his damnedest to ignore the sudden, unbidden heat that scorched his fingers as his palm felt the seat and the top of his hand slid across her firm thigh and soft buttock.

Mind over matter, he told himself. *Get your mind off her matter.* He pulled out the belt and laid it across her tiny waist, doing his best, with fingers as deft as an experienced surgeon's, not to touch any part of her. He knew another touch would undo him, make him want more, and that wouldn't be good for either his future or his emotional and physical well-being.

It didn't matter what Myrna said. Between him and the Mags there would be nothing but a chaste kiss, and a platonic relationship. He may have been accepted by the in-laws, but he was still the gardener's son, the man who would always be second-class in the heart and mind of Margaret O'Brien St. James. And he'd best remind himself of that fact during this New York trip. Often.

Finally, with minimal fumbling, the belt hit home. He jerked the excess material tight around her, heard her let out a puff of that sweet breath, which brought another wave of hunger through him. He grabbed the *Newsweek* some person with foresight had left stuck in the seat pocket, and placed it over his lap, covering the evidence of his weakness for Mags.

He needed a code word. Something he could say to himself that would take his mind off her whenever he found himself slipping. Some word that would make him forget how Mags's hand felt in his, how her scent aroused him, how touching her once, twice, made him want to touch more.

Warts.

"So," John asked, going for the nonchalant approach. "Feeling better now?"

"Do you hear those noises?"

"You mean the banging below? They're loading the luggage."

"I knew that." Her blue-veined knuckles gripped the hand-rest as one loud, thumping noise followed another. The floor of the plane vibrated under their feet. "Hennessey, my problem has always been that I analyze too much. At Rice, the professors liked my questions, but in high school, they were quite distressed with me. You see, I start thinking of all the various possibilities. What if they forget to latch the door? What if the door flies open and the luggage falls out?"

"You know that won't happen."

"No, I don't know. Anything can happen."

"Mags, why are you thinking these things?"

"I'm contemplating." Her voice seemed to get stronger. "I can see it all now. The door flies open, the pressure inside the plane builds until all the airplane nails pop out, all the rivets unrivet, all the panels tear apart, and then the plane, and all the people, like you and me, disintegrate into thin air, and there won't be anything left."

"That won't happen," he repeated with calm certainty.

She crossed her arms under her breasts and gave him one of her superior smiles, as if she knew something the rest of the world didn't. That smile unsettled him.

"It's a good thing I gave all my jewelry to Essie this afternoon. It's good to think ahead, take care of business."

"I hope you thought of a way to get your stash back

from your sister when we get home. She didn't look like she'd be anxious to take off all that gold.''

Mags waved a dismissive hand. "I really don't think that will happen.''

"Which part? Getting the jewelry back, or us getting back?''

Again she gave him that don't-you-wish-you-knew-what-I-know smile. "You're the one who thinks he's the next Peter Jennings. Why don't you take a stab at inferring the conclusion.''

"You want me to do what?''

"Just guess." She blew out a breath and sighed.

A loud noise cut through the cabin. The plane rolled forward. "Ohmygod!" Mags's eyelids shut tight. "What's going on?''

"Why don't you open your eyes, look around and," he added sarcastically, "infer the conclusion.''

Her eyes popped open. With a toss of her head, and a voice although shaky, remarkably professional, she said, "The plane's backing out. There's no rearview mirrors so it's impossible for me to see what's coming behind us. Therefore, if the pilot needed my help navigating, I couldn't give it to him.''

"I would bet hard cash that the pilot will get along fine without your help.''

"But you don't know that for sure, do you?''

Her eyes closed again, her hands clutched the seat handles and she chanted serenely, *"Now I lay me down to sleep, death will come, I will not weep.''*

"Contemplating again? Or prophesying?''

"And when we become a mere puff of smoke, you'll be sorry for the fun you poked.''

"Ah, contemplating." The jet engines roared.

"And if I die before I wake, I pray John lands in the deepest lake.''

"You called me John.''

"I'm going to throw up.''

"No. Don't do that," he ordered. "Breathe deep."

"I can't."

"Magpie, we're only taxiing. We're not off the ground yet."

A loud grinding sound, gears gnashing against gears, came from the first-class section. The plane lurched forward, then resumed its normal bumpy pace down the runway.

"You know he's speeding," she said matter-of-factly.

"He's taxiing," he told her.

"He should slow down. You'd think he'd know about runway collisions."

"I don't even know about runway collisions." Where was she getting this stuff? "If he goes any slower than the five miles an hour we're going, we'll be stopped."

"That's my point. I'm having a heart attack. Angina. Stroke. Blocked aorta." Her voice was wispy but urgent. "The pilot needs to stop now and call a doctor. Now!" Both her hands bunched the silk material over her right breast.

"Your heart's on the left."

She switched sides. Then switched back again. "My heart's beating so fast it jumped over."

"Magpie, what am I going to do with you?" He shook his head slowly. He reached for her hands, now ice, and enclosed them in his warm grip. She let him hold on to her and didn't try to get away. He liked that. She found some comfort in his touch.

For the first time since the night he walked out of her house, he felt as if he had something to offer, something that she needed that no one else could give her. His protection. "You're going to be fine. Nothing's going to happen."

Her smooth skin crinkled over tightly closed eyes. "Do you hear that noise?" Noise became a six-syllable word.

"The air-conditioning system was just activated."

"Then it's not working. The electrical system must be out. It's hot in here. I'm so hot I could die."

Mags twisted from the waist up until she faced him. She pulled her hands out of his and grabbed the front of his shirt, pulling him down to her with a strength he'd never thought she had. "The plane's on fire," she said. "Do you smell it?"

He pried her fingers loose and once again enclosed them inside his own. "It's your imagination."

"No, it's not." She cocked her head to the side. "I need to listen for unusual sounds. My hearing is excellent, and I might hear something the flight attendants miss. The pilot can't hear anything up there. He won't know if the wings are broken. See—" she pointed out the window "—there's a crack."

"It's the wing flap."

"Ohmygod. They need a new wing."

Three flight attendants stood at strategic points down the airplane, holding up oxygen masks, while from somewhere a feminine voice came through the loudspeaker, telling the captive audience which strings to pull in case of an emergency.

Mags gazed at the back of the seat in front of her. "You're going to live and I'm going to die."

He squeezed her hand. "This is silly."

"Because when the plane goes down, that flight attendant, the one in the middle, is going to hand you the oxygen mask and make sure you'll live."

"Don't act stupid."

"Oh, really?" Her eyebrow shot up. "I know you, Hennessey. When the plane loses oxygen, you won't think to share your mask with me."

"You'll never know, will you?" He grinned wickedly.

"Flight crew, prepare for takeoff," the pilot's voice came over the intercom.

The attendants walked away, taking their oxygen masks

with them. The normally strong, savvy woman next to him began to breathe hard and heavy, gasping for air.

"The plane's taking on power," she said, the words speeding together.

"That's right."

"This is our last chance," she warned as the engines came to life and the plane charged down the runway. Then slowed.

Mags took her hand back, reached up and pressed the call button over her head. Two flight attendants, both strapped in their seats, glanced in their direction. One held up her finger, mouthing the words, "One minute."

"Mags, what are you doing?"

"Don't stop me. I've got to protect us. I'm not doing this just for me." She rushed her words. "I'm doing this for everyone. I told you, I had a vision. You weren't listening to me again."

"Mags, Mags." He shook her arm. "Slow down."

The jet gathered speed again, then braked.

Before he could stop her, she had her seat belt unfastened.

"Something's wrong. I can tell. It's my duty as a citizen of the United States to protect everyone on this plane. I gave you a chance to be a hero, and you didn't jump at it."

"Get your seat belt back on." He tried to gather the straps and link the clip together.

Once again the plane gathered speed, the engines rumbling, then all became quiet and still.

Mags popped up. "That does it."

"Sit down," John ordered, taking hold of her arm. "You're getting hysterical."

"How dare you? I'll not sit by passively while this sorry excuse for an airplane tries to get off the ground."

"Listen to me. I'll help you through this. I'll tell you what every noise is, every sound. I promise you'll be okay." And if it turned out she was right and they crashed, none of his promises would matter anyway. If she was wrong, then he would be a hero.

Mags looked up at him, her blue eyes clear and determined. He let down his guard, thinking she had come to her senses. Suddenly, without warning, she stood and flung out her arms.

Gathering a lungful of prepressurized air, she screamed, "Stop the plane—I'm getting off!"

6

PASSENGERS TWISTED and turned their heads in Margaret's direction. "It's okay, everyone." She waved at them, and smiled as best she could over shivering teeth. "Everything's fine." Or at least it would be once the pilot made a U-turn and brought her back where she belonged. She felt bad, she really did. She didn't want to ruin everyone's good time, but no one could possibly understand the blinding fear she felt. No one knew how her insides were ready to burst through her skin. No one.

She tried to climb over Hennessey's steel legs, but her skirt was tight and straight and hindered her progress. "I knew I should have taken the aisle seat," she said through clenched teeth.

"You weren't conscious enough to make that decision," he said.

Hennessey kept reaching for her, and did that man ever have hands. Large, strong and powerful. She was quick though, and didn't get caught. The blood pumping through her veins gave her strength to keep moving forward. Fear did that to a person, gave them inhuman strength.

Hennessey's hands circled her waist and brought her back to her seat. "She'll be fine," he said, addressing the passengers around them. His hand went underneath her, and she heard him mumbling something about warts. Warts. It figures. The physical side of her heart beat faster at his touch, while the emotional part plummeted at the thought of what he felt as he touched her. Warts.

Well, she'd had enough. Warts indeed. She shot back up from her seat. "Let me out of here."

Unfortunately she didn't have enough strength to hurl herself across Hennessey's mighty leg roadblock. Finally, she gathered all the St. James pride she could find and tried a completely different approach. Superiority. As she glared down at him, she said haughtily, "This was a nice little way to spend the afternoon. Sorry, but I have to leave you now." She fluttered several fingers in the direction of his nose. "If you'll be so kind—" One red-dagger nail stopped waving and pointed down to his Herculean thighs. "Move the tree trunks."

His forehead wrinkled as he tried to interpret her words. Great. This was not the time for Hennessey to start thinking. "Please, Hennessey, I'm sure once I make my way up to the cockpit and discuss the situation with the pilots, we'll be heading right back to the terminal. Then, if you wish, you can continue without me."

"Oh no you don't, Magpie. Sit yourself down." He finally got his hands on her waist and pushed her into her seat. Swatting at those long fingers didn't do much good. Hennessey was strong.

Linda the flight attendant who, up until that moment, had seemed to be relatively friendly and reasonable, lurched from her safety seat and rushed over to them.

"Are you scared?" Linda's smile of gentle understanding and her hazel eyes filled with sympathy were in direct contrast to her locked arms, which added extra weight to Hennessey's already-iron grip.

"Scared? Me? Of course not." Margaret tried to clear the lump that had taken up permanent residence in her throat. After a few unsuccessful attempts, she finally squeaked, "Please let me off," as she got to her feet once more.

Linda's slender body was still large enough to block the exit. "That's not possible. Why don't you sit back down."

Margaret sat, heard a small mewling sound and was suddenly aware that pathetic cry had come from her. She closed her eyes and made up another mantra, "Where there's a will, I'll make a way. I won't be scared. Being afraid is for other people, not for me. I'm bigger than that. I can make it."

"Will she be all right now?" asked the hovering Linda.

"She'll be fine." Hennessey gave the flight attendant that charming smile Margaret was quickly learning to despise. He had his hands under her again, searching for the seat belt, and kept mumbling "warts."

"Mr. Hennessey?" Linda had a puzzled look on her face.

Margaret knew she must look humiliated.

"I'll take care of her," he said.

"Are you sure?" Linda asked.

"Positive. She'll get over it."

Margaret punched Hennessey in the arm as hard as she could. "There's nothing to get over," she called out to Linda's retreating back, then turned on Hennessey. "Don't call me names."

"I don't know what you're talking about."

A wart by any other name— She wouldn't say another word. Not one more. She hated everything. The way he thought of her as some kind of epidermal virus. The horrible fear that had overcome her, that had taken control of her life, that had reduced her to nothing more than a squeamish mass of whimpering—warts?

He would always think of her as a dud. The stud and the dud. A dud not even worth saving. "Linda took the spare oxygen mask with her."

"You know as well as I do that the mask comes from above. You also know that statistically you won't need it."

"Right. Who needs oxygen right before a plane blows up, or crashes, or sinks? What good is it going to do you if you're already in a million pieces?"

"It's not going to happen."

Her lips trembled and she couldn't stop them. Her eyes

were blinking and twitching and she couldn't still them, either.

Hennessey's finger gently wiped the moisture traveling down her cheeks. "I'm not crying." She sniffed in righteous indignation.

"Of course not."

"As long as we understand that."

He nodded, gently wiping the other cheek with the pad of his thumb.

"Here—" Without waiting for permission, he took both her hands in his and held her cold fingers securely.

"Why are you being so nice to me?"

"I like you, Magpie. I always have and you know that."

"No, I didn't." She shook her head, more to get rid of the water brimming in her eyes than to disagree with him. She wouldn't let him see her cry again. She had already shown him how vulnerable, how weak she was, and she had to gather up what little pride she had left.

The last time she'd felt so vulnerable was almost three years ago, when he'd walked out on her. "You're only trying to be nice because you know that no matter what you say to me now, it won't matter. After the plane crashes, I won't be around later to tell the viewing public how really nice you are in person. Even if you call me a wart."

"I didn't call you a wart."

"I heard you. How do you think I feel when you say that?" She slugged him on the arm again. "In front of Linda yet?"

"Ouch. Cut that out." Then he started to laugh. First softly, then loudly, from deep in his chest.

"What's so funny?" The man was sick.

"You are. Put yourself in my place. If you were me, and you had to stick your hand under a woman's bottom, not once, not twice, but at least three times, well…what would you be thinking?"

"You think my rear end's like a wart?"

"It's my code word. Like men who think about baseball so they don't—well, you know."

"No, I don't know. Explain." O-o-o-h, she couldn't wait to hear him get out of this one.

"Forget it. Let's just say that when my hands are on you, if I say 'wart,' I won't think about other things."

Men were so primal.

Then he took her hands again, and tightened his hold as the engines began to hum, first softly, then louder and louder. This time they roared into action and didn't stop as they had before. Now she didn't care if he was mumbling wart-wart-wart, she just didn't want him to let go of her.

The seats and walls shook. The lights in the cabin flashed off and on then stayed off. The airplane moved down the runway, gathering speed, faster and faster, the momentum pushing Margaret back in the seat.

She shut her eyes as tight as she could, and still small tears, one drop at a time, managed to escape and fall down her cheeks. Her hands began to shake uncontrollably within the tight cocoon of Hennessey's grasp. He let her go for only a second, just long enough to slip his arm around her shoulders and pull her body close to his warmth, before taking hold of her hands again.

"Open your eyes and look outside," he said.

"I can't."

"We're off the ground."

She moaned.

Linda stopped in front of them. "Can I get you something to drink? We'll be pulling the cart through in a moment, but I'll be happy to get you something now."

Hennessey let Margaret's hands go, and she quickly folded them in her lap, trying to keep them from shaking. "No, thank you."

Hennessey smiled at Linda. "Beer for me, a Sprite or 7UP, or whatever you have, for Mags here."

"I can't drink anything." She turned toward the window,

saw nothing but blue skies and white clouds and turned away again.

"Listen, Magpie," he said as he rubbed both his hands over hers, not letting go. "If you think flying in this airplane is something to get scared about, you don't know what fear is. You should have some guy named Fang anxious to rearrange your face."

"I don't know why you'd be afraid. All you'd have to do is call him a wart."

"It's not quite the same thing. Fang and his famous twelve-inch dagger weren't put off that easily. Rumor was, the guy kept a body count under the Brazos River. He was after me. That's why I quit school. To make sure I lived."

She looked at Hennessey. Raw, virile, potent man. Telling her stories that probably weren't true. "I know why you're telling me this. You want me to think that your fear was bigger than mine and you got over it."

"No. I'm telling you that one day I ran into Fang, with his dagger, and he didn't kill me. It was my cowardliness that caused me to drop out of school, to let it rule my life. I didn't need to do that."

The pilot came over the speakers, his voice crackling, weaving in and out. "We're at our cruising altitude of thirty-two thousand feet. I'm going to leave the seat-belt sign on as we fly over Arkansas, Missouri, Illinois, Indiana, Ohio, Pennsylvania and into New York. There are a few storms up ahead, but we'll try to get you through them as smoothly as possible. Have a good trip, everyone. Relax. The flight crew will be around with drinks and a snack."

The airplane dipped about one hundred feet. Margaret caught her breath, and groaned painfully. "We're going to die."

Her eyelashes did butterfly flutters that had his gut twisted inside. He remembered once, a long, long time ago, when he'd kissed those eyelashes closed, when he'd had his lips on hers and had felt the beginnings of her burning fire. Mags, ice queen on the outside, an inferno smoldering on the inside. He had once, it seemed so long ago, come close to knowing the complete, fiery Magpie. But his own pride had made him walk out. Maybe he'd been wrong.

Maybe he'd been the coward when it came to relationships. When it came to her.

He knew she had a soft side. A tender, compassionate side. He'd found that out by accident one day, snooping through her desk drawers, looking for her stash of Milky Ways. In the bottom drawer, hidden underneath the candy, were letters from women she'd helped at the county's battered women's center. More letters, written in almost childlike letters, from adults she had taught to read.

John hadn't known about this side of her, and he'd never mentioned what he found out, either. He closed the drawer and left her cubicle, leaving without a chocolate bar.

The airplane dropped again, his stomach stayed in the air, and Mags let loose with another scream.

"Okay, let's forget the F-word—fear—and talk about the T-word—turbulence," he said.

Her watery voice agreed.

"Turbulence is flying through the air on currents, much like a boat in the ocean goes over the waves."

Her skin had gone from pale to ghostly. She fumbled in the seat pocket in front of her as she made little hiccuping noises. She pulled out flight instructions, magazines and chewing-gum wrappers and scattered them over him and the floor. When she got hold of the little paper doggie bag, she popped it open and shoved her face inside.

"Ah, geez. Not that. Willie! Willie!" John yelled, reaching across the seat back, slapping the cameraman on the side of the head. "Help me."

"I'm not sick." Mags muffled voice came from inside the bag.

Willie twisted around and focused immediately on her. "Way cool, man." He climbed over the man sitting in the aisle seat next to him, with camcorder in hand, red light on, mike open and lens shoved toward the bag. She pulled her head out, and the camera recorded fear, embarrassment and humiliation for the whole state of Texas to see.

"Shut the damn camera off," John snarled.

"No way, José," Willie said.

"I'm not sick. Just nauseated."

"Can't you get sick?" Willie asked. "Throwing up makes good news."

John shoved the camcorder aside.

"Hey, whatcha do that for? The *Grapevine* pays good for something like this."

"You're a dead man." John started to rise from his seat, his hands going for Willie's throat.

"Hey, get back." Willie looked at him for a moment and said in complete sincerity, "You need a life. You know ratings are the game and if Margaret throws up, it's my windfall." The camera zoomed in closer again.

"I'm not sick, I tell you." Mags's eyes grew wide in horror when she realized Willie wanted her to humiliate herself for his own gain.

Linda rushed over with a cold wet cloth. John took it, placing it on Mags's hot forehead.

"Gosh, Margaret, I thought we were friends. The least you could have done..."

Willie clutched the camera, and the people around them stared with their eyes and mouths wide-open as John's threats turned vivid and lively. Finally, Willie climbed back to his seat, muttering, "Management bloodsuckers. Creativity squashers. Money robbers. Keeping a man from earning an honest dollar."

Linda said, "There's a number of empty seats in the back. You two could have some privacy for the rest of the trip."

Fear rose from Margaret's pores. "You want me to walk down the airplane? While it's moving?"

"I'll hold your hand, Mags." John reached for hers. "You'll be fine."

She didn't respond for a moment, and John wasn't sure

she would. But then she sent him a smile, a brief, heart-stopping tilt of her lips, and he knew if the plane's door opened right at this moment, he would be able to walk on clouds. He sent a silent prayer of thanks to the powers that be, then took her icy hand.

"Thank you," she said, her voice chattering. "For being so kind."

"I'm not being kind. I'm just being me," John said.

"I was talking to Linda."

Mags may have been joking or she may have been serious, but either way, it was the first sign of life he'd seen in her.

Linda chattered as they made their way toward the back of the plane. "People get scared all the time. It's the stress of going up, the bumps, the air currents—it does something to the stomach. You should have seen the guy on my last plane. Looked like Sylvester Stallone, all muscles and real macho. Cried the whole trip. Ms. St. James, you're doing way better than that guy did."

After they were seated in the last row, Mags looked up at Linda, and said, "I don't know how to thank you for all your help."

She patted Mags's shoulder. "Well, you could invite me to the wedding."

John interrupted, "Sure. November twenty-seventh, at the studio. We'd love to have you."

"Really?"

"Sure. Right, Mags?"

"Yes, we would." She nodded her head slowly.

After Linda left, she turned to John. "Why did you invite her?"

"Because we will do what we have to do to get the ratings up to first place. If it means going along with Sid's plan, we'll do it. Remember, Magpie, it's all a game."

"Yes. All a game." She didn't look happy. "Hennessey?"

"John."

"What?"

"I want you to call me John. Or honey, or sweetheart. Or sugar. Better yet, call me lover-boy."

"Are you crazy?" Her head tilted back as she looked up at him. Her mouth set in a perfect, kissable pout.

"And when you say lover-boy, do it with that little growl you use. It's so damn sexy, it drives me nuts. Like, 'You lover-boy you.'" He tried to imitate her. "I get excited all over, if you know what I mean, when I hear you talk like that."

Mags's face turned bright red. "I will not call you lover-boy. Or anything else. I'll call you Hennessey."

He let out a long, dejected sigh. "If you must. But lover-boy seemed so…so…right."

"And you can call me Margaret."

"Not Mags?"

"Margaret."

"Not my little Magpie?"

"Margaret."

"How about Toot? As in, 'You toot my horn.'"

"Maggie. How would that be? A lot of people call me Maggie."

"All right, all right." He knew who those people were, since he'd read the letters in her bottom drawer. His heart tightened a notch. Calling her Maggie was an honor. "Maggie then. I would never argue with my future wife."

"Remember that."

"Especially a pseudowife who has bad luck following her around."

The airplane's engines groaned and it seemed as if it was struggling to move through the air.

Mags's face immediately paled again. "I know. I just know we're going to die. I can feel it in my bones."

"So, do you want to tell me what happened in Chicago that caused this life-altering change in your behavior?"

"Are you trying to distract me again?"

"Yes. Is it working?"

"No. But I'll tell you anyway." She paused for a moment, then said, "You know I used to be the travel reporter for WLS. Well, my feeling is three times and you're out. My first close call was when I had to take a small prop plane." She pointed two index fingers straight ahead and made swirling gestures.

"A two-propeller job."

She nodded. "I had an interview to do in Louisiana with this alligator handler. The plane lost an engine."

"Did he find it again?"

"Not while I was on the plane. We landed on the only solid ground in the middle of a marshy bayou, and it wasn't all that solid. The plane sunk halfway into the water. The man I was supposed to interview rowed out to where we were and rescued us. I had to do mouth-to-mouth on the pilot. Not that he was hurt. He'd fainted."

"Okay, that was one, and you made it. What was two?"

"Michigan. I had finished a story about a woman who lived in a lighthouse and thought she was the beacon."

"What?"

"Mrs. Muldune did kind of light up. Maybe it was suggestive power or something. Anyway, at the airport, we had boarded the plane to take us to Chicago. The weather was terrible—snow, sleet, hail—but the tower gave us clearance to go, and we did. We would have been fine, if we'd taken off right then. But the pilot had to wait for the runway to clear, and didn't realize the wings had iced up again."

"He didn't take off, did he?"

"Well, just a little. He kind of crashed down again. The wheels came off, and we did a belly flop on the pavement."

John gazed at her golden-blond hair, the pair of guileless, big blue eyes, and lips he was finding harder and harder to resist kissing, no matter how many times he said "wart" silently in his head. He pushed back a flyaway pale strand of hair off her cheek, supreme control keeping him from cupping her face in his hands, bringing those lips to his and kissing her until she fainted.

The pilot's voice came through the sound system again. "Well, folks, sorry for the bumpy ride. Wanted to point out a few sites. We're passing over Notre Dame, my alma mater."

"Don't you see, Hennessey? I shouldn't be on this plane."

Maggie had her gaze focused on his lips, and without realizing what he was doing, he moistened his, readying them.

The airplane rocked from side to side.

"That was only two. You said three." He lowered his mouth toward hers.

"We're on three."

"Scared?" He wasn't talking about airplanes.

She half closed her eyes and lifted her mouth closer to his. "Terrified."

He pulled back.

So did she and softly whimpered, "I didn't think I'd make it the last time. I didn't think I could be saved."

"I'm not here to save you, either, Maggie."

She leaned toward him this time as if searching for his warmth, needing his closeness.

"I know."

"I can't protect you from the future, either," he said. "Or protect myself."

"I know that now, too."

He needed to look in her eyes. "We're going to be alone for four days. You could get hurt." He could get hurt.

She put her hand around his neck, pushing her fingers through his hair. "I've been hurt."

Her touch almost undid him, only his control, the control that was slowly slipping away, kept him from doing to her what he had been dreaming about for months. For years.

"I need a chance, too," Maggie squealed as the plane took another dip.

He descended upon her lips, capturing her mouth, taking what he needed, giving her back what he hoped she craved.

Her mouth softened, opened, ready to receive him. He tasted her, explored her, and longed for more.

Seconds turned into minutes. Minutes passed too quickly. He reached under her silk blouse, feeling soft skin. He moved his hand higher. She groaned into his mouth. He touched the fullness of her breast, felt her nipple harden beneath his hand and the lace barely containing her full, ripe breasts.

The talkative pilot came through the speakers again. "We're passing over the Liberty Bell, folks, heading into New York State."

Maggie pressed her body closer to him as the airplane jolted them, rocked them and pushed them into each other.

His mouth became one with hers, kissing, teasing. His tongue explored the enticing softness of her, devouring her sweetness. Time had no meaning. The rain pelting down on the wings only heightened the beating of his racing heart.

Her hands kneaded his neck, his shoulders. She slipped them under the material of his shirt, her cold skin being warmed by the heat of his body. He had her as close to him as he could. As close as decency would allow. He wanted more, needed more, and as much as he tried to get his mind off her by repeating his code word in his head, nothing worked. He couldn't stop thinking about Mags. Maggie.

The pilot's voice crackled through the loudspeaker into the cabin once again. "On your left you'll see the Statue of Liberty."

Margaret broke the kiss, her face again turning ghostly white. The passengers had become quiet, the plane rocked and shook between the clouds on its descent. The lights in the cabin went off.

"Folks, hope you had a pleasant ride. Sorry about the turbulence. New York is a balmy sixty-eight degrees today. Flight crew, prepare for landing."

Tears formed in Maggie's eyes. She gripped his hand,

digging her fingernails into his palms. "Thank you. Thank you for kissing me all over the United States, and making me forget we were in the air."

"It was nothing. Any guy would have done the same thing."

The tears didn't stop flowing as the airplane jolted. Oh, hell. He did what any man would have done under the circumstances. He swooped down and kissed her again, wanting her to forget her fear. He captured her lips and tongue and didn't let go.

The distraction worked, too. She didn't seem to realize they'd landed until they were safely taxiing to the gate.

"I told you flying was fun. And safe," John said, thinking warts-warts-warts. There was no way he could stand up right now. His body needed to cool down. His heart had to stop racing.

"How can I ever thank you?" Maggie began to babble, gathering her purse, talking fast, pushing words out of her mouth. "I know you were only kissing me to keep my mind off this silly fear I have, and I appreciate that. Please don't feel that you have to ever do this again. I'm fine now."

"Right." John's lips lifted into a wolfish grin. "I did this all for you." She had to be kidding. "Let's get out of here, grab a cab, check in at the hotel and I'll see if I can get tickets for the Knicks game."

"Oh no, I can't do that." Maggie shook her head and tried to pull away.

"Why not?" The word *no* was not part of his fantasy.

Maggie opened her purse and dangled her gold American Express card. "I have to shop."

"Shop?" What did she want to do that for? "You may never get to see another live basketball game here in New York."

"I need underwear." She smiled shyly. "And I need to be by myself."

"You're not going shopping, are you? You're going to cash in your return ticket for a train ride," he accused.

"I can't believe you'd think that." She sounded affronted at the notion.

"Maggie?"

"You have to trust me."

"Trust? You?"

She grinned at him. Sweet, sexy, devilish. That grin said it all.

No way was he letting her out of his sight.

7

As Maggie disembarked from the airplane, she knew her life had changed forever. She'd told Hennessey to call her Maggie. The only other people who called her by that name were the adults she taught to read at Houston Community College, and the abused women she counseled at the county's women's center.

When he'd kissed her, she never once thought about planes crashing. How could she have? His kisses had had her flying higher than any airplane.

Too bad she was taking the train back. She'd miss those Hennessey airplane kisses. If they never kissed each other again, she'd always remember the way his lips felt on hers, the way his tongue captured hers, searched, explored, stroked and demanded attention. He had left her breathless. He had left her wanting more. Needing more.

She was smart enough to know he'd only kissed her because he'd felt sorry for her, because he was probably worried if he didn't have his mouth over hers, she'd scream. As far as he was concerned, she was sure, kissing her was done for purely selfish reasons. If they hadn't been on an airplane, those kisses would never have taken place.

Hennessey carried his duffel bag, and she held on to her purse. New York's cool November air whistled through the canvas walkway, raising goose bumps on her arms. Hennessey flipped his duffel bag over his shoulder and pulled her closer to his side, putting an arm around her, sharing the warmth of his body.

The inside of the terminal building wasn't much warmer.

People scurried through the corridors, going one way or another, bumping into her, pushing her even closer to Hennessey.

Willie still walked backward, as he had since they disembarked the plane. "So, how's your stomach, Margaret?" he asked.

"You take your job too seriously," Maggie said, shivering.

The camera aimed at her face. "Sid the main man's depending on me."

Hennessey leaned down, whispering in her ear, "Since when does anyone care what Sid wants?"

"You must." Maggie shivered again as the warmth of his breath reached her neck. "We're here."

"I'm here because I want to be here. Remember that. Sid gave me the opportunity, but I wouldn't have taken it if I didn't want it."

"So you've said."

Willie called out, stumbling over his untied, frayed shoelaces. "Tell the viewers back home how it feels to be in New York."

"It's great!" John tightened his arm around Maggie's shoulder. "Me and Maggie are looking forward to reporting our visit to everyone back home."

Maggie—that name coming from Hennessey's lips sounded like a promise.

"And how about you, Margaret?" Willie asked. "What're your first impressions of New York?"

John slipped his arm from her shoulders to her waist, and before she had a chance to alienate the people in the city where he planned to spend the rest of his life, he squeezed her waist hard.

"Ouch!" she squealed.

"Being in New York has left her speechless." John sent the viewers his loopy grin.

"I'm never speechless," she argued through the tight smile she gave the camcorder. "I'm looking forward to getting to the Beckendorf Hotel. I simply adore the quaintness of a bed-and-breakfast. In fact, renovated houses are a hobby of mine, since I'm living in one in Sugar Land. I'm looking forward to talking to the owners, getting tips on stripping floors, wallpaper, antique furniture. I'm sure New York will be a wonderful, educational experience.''

Willie turned off the camera. ''I'll get the rest of the equipment from baggage and head for the hotel,'' he said. ''I'm scheduled to do location shots, so I won't see you again until tonight at the dinner Sid set up.''

''The dinner's at eight tonight,'' John said. ''Try not to get too distracted, and forget to show up.''

Willie scrunched his face together and pointed to his scrawny chest. ''Moi? Miss out on free food? Hey, I need to overnight this tape, and then I'll be there. No prob-lem-o.'' He headed down the terminal, stopped and came back to them. ''Margaret, can I ask you something?''

''Sure, Willie.''

''Who told you the Beckendorf was a bed-and-breakfast?''

''Sid mentioned it.''

''Okeydokey.'' The cameraman had a twisted smirk on his face. ''See ya.''

''What's with him?'' Maggie asked.

''A past consisting of too many illegal drugs.''

''Willie?''

''Ah, Maggie, Maggie. For such a worldly babe, you're naive.''

They passed through the doors and walked toward the taxi stand.

John took in a big gulp of air. A strong, fisted hand shot through the air. ''Maggie!'' he shouted to the sky. ''I love New York!''

''How do you know?'' she asked in a dry monotone. ''You haven't even been out of the airport.''

''Doesn't matter. I feel it, right here in my gut. New

York City and John Patrick Hennessey were made for each other.''

She lowered her gaze to the sidewalk. Two tufts of sickly green grass were making a valiant effort to poke through one of the many cracks in the concrete. Paper cups, discarded pages of newspapers and other trash floated past them in the wind.

''What do you see when you look out here?'' she asked.

''A city full of vibrant people.''

''You mean crowds.''

''Streets paved in gold.''

''Streets full of trash.''

''Air with its own unique fragrance.''

''That's dead fish you're smelling, Hennessey.''

''Beautiful blue skies.''

''Gray smog.''

''Now, Maggie, aren't you ever happy?'' He grabbed her arm. ''Come on.'' They hurried down the long line of parked taxis until they reached the first cab. He opened the back door and waited for her to get in.

''I'm always happy. Or I was until this morning.'' She took the inside handle and tried to close the door. ''Thanks, Hennessey. Thanks for everything. I'll see you later at the Beckendorf.'' Again she pulled the handle and still it wouldn't budge.

He smiled down at her, not saying a word.

''I'll see you at the hotel later this afternoon,'' she repeated. ''When you register, please get me a nonsmoking room with a private bath. You know how those converted houses are. You have to ask for private baths. If Sid didn't cover the expense, I'll pick up the difference.''

Still nothing but a sly grin.

''Until later,'' she said, pulling on the door handle again.

''I'm going with you.''

''No you're not. I've got to get—'' she lowered her voice ''—personal things.''

A very male, very lecherous grin appeared on his face. "I'm an expert in women's underwear."

She battled for the door. "So am I."

The cabdriver yelled in broken English, "We go now."

"We're getting married. Any new underwear you get is now a group decision."

"Get lost, Hennessey."

"Not on your life." He leaned into the cab, both hands grasping the roof. "How can you be afraid to get on an airplane, but have no fear driving around with a New York cabbie? It doesn't make sense."

The cabdriver turned, and again yelled, "Cab go."

"I'm on solid ground now." Leaning over the front seat, she ordered the driver, "Grand Central Station, driver."

"What?" John threw the duffel in the front seat next to the driver and shoved his way into the back, giving Maggie no choice but to move over or get sat on. "The Beckendorf."

She elbowed him in the ribs, and reordered, "Grand Central."

"What do you want to go there for? Play tennis? Eat at the oyster bar? Take a tour?"

Her lips barely moved as she said, "I'm cashing in my plane ticket and buying a train ticket."

"We'll discuss that later. We've got four days to talk about it." John wedged closer to her side, drinking in the scent of her flowery shampoo, her spicy-sweet perfume.

"There's nothing to talk about." Her nose went right up in the air.

He was getting to enjoy that pointed nose. He was even getting to enjoy being near Maggie, which, he realized, could either be good or bad depending on a guy's outlook. Right now his outlook was definitely subjective. Her nearness, the rubbing of clothed arms and hips and softly toned muscles was enough to turn even a stronger man than him—and he was plenty strong—into mush. "Beckendorf, and no detour."

The driver pulled out into traffic and headed toward the skyline. "Yes, mister. I listen to the man."

"Oooh." Maggie's stormy blue eyes spit sparks before she looked down at her hands folded in her lap. "I can't take the plane back." Her voice caught.

That fear of hers was coming back. She couldn't go on like this.

"Try not to think about that right now." Maybe by the time they left, her fear would be gone, too.

"I've already thought about it. That's all I've thought about. And then I came up with a plan. I'm taking a train back."

"Not good. Did I ever tell you about the time I was on a train that derailed in Carbondale, Illinois?"

Maggie's pink lips formed an "O," and just as her perfectly arched eyebrows were creasing together, he could swear he saw a seventy-watt lightbulb flash over her head.

"Okay, no trains." She flung her arm pointing to the left. "Driver, take me to the bus station."

The driver not so subtly cursed her in several recognizable languages, including English.

"What's his problem?" Maggie delicately shrugged.

"The Beckendorf," John reordered in the whiskey-smooth TV-announcer voice he used to sell hair color to graying bachelors. "Nowhere else."

The driver sputtered, "Mixed-up tourists. No minds. Stupid-o. Nuts-o."

"No tip-o if you don't get us to the hotel in one piece-o. And without the commentary," John said.

Screeching tires whirled around corners. Horns honked in offensive unison.

John put his arm around the back of the seat and leaned his shoulder into hers. He enjoyed touching her. He liked the way she felt, all soft and womanly. He couldn't wait until they reached the hotel. He leaned back, slow and lazylike, and asked, "Now, Maggie, where do you get these cockeyed ideas of yours?"

"Cockeyed? How dare you say that?"

"Touchy?" He grinned.

She scooted away from him. He followed her across the seat.

"I'm thinking of my safety. My life."

"Would I let you endanger your life? No way in hell. I'm thinking of your safety, too. Buses are big. They've been known to get their wheels stuck when they go over railroad tracks. What do you think happens when a train is speeding down the tracks, and the bus is stuck—" John slapped his hands together, and said, "*Bam!* Accordion steel."

"Hennessey!"

"Broken bodies, oil, toxic gases."

"Hennessey!"

"What? You're a reporter." He shrugged. "You know it's a mess."

Maggie's breath came in rapid bursts until suddenly, she stopped breathing completely. He lowered his lips toward her, intent on resuscitation. To his disappointment, she pushed him away and a smile burst on her face as she joyfully announced, "I'll go home on a cruise ship."

"Remember the *Titanic*," he warned, lowering his lips again.

She scooted closer to the door. "What's wrong with you?" Her practical St. James self burst forward. "Get realistic."

"Now, now, sweet Magpie. I am. Now how about a kiss?"

"No."

"Yes." He leaned across the seat, reached the shell of her ear and nipped gently, his own breath catching when he felt her shiver in response. He caressed her shoulder, bringing her nearer to him, nibbling her earlobe, wanting to get as close to her as possible. This was a dangerous game he played, only try as he might, he couldn't stop himself. "Let's see how real I've been today," he teased. "Let me count the ways."

"No, don't."

"I kissed you until you forgot you were on an airplane over at least four different states, but who's counting?"

"I kissed you back," she stated. "We're even."

She looked too cute, too righteous. A deadly combination for a man as worked up as he was. "No, we're not even yet. But I know how we can be." He nibbled the curve of her neck.

"You don't play fair." She moaned softly, tilting her head to give him easier access. "I can't compete with you at this."

He sat back up and smiled down at her flushed face. She smiled back at him. He was feeling expansive. Generous. Maybe he'd even break out his own gold card. "Sure you can. For all my generosity on the plane, keeping you distracted, entertained, sacrificing what I had planned to do—"

"What was that?"

"Double-check my résumé. Add anything to it that I may have forgotten. You owe me my studying time. And this is how you'll pay."

He wanted to laugh at her doubtful, distrustful expression. He had a long way to go to get her to trust him. "A Knicks game tonight."

"We have a dinner to attend tonight," she said, sounding relieved. "You knew when we left Houston that I had to go shopping when I got here."

Sure he knew. But he couldn't let her out of his sight. She'd already all but told him that she'd bolt. "Boy, Maggie, you're really going to owe me now." He let out a long, resigned sigh. "I'll have to make the ultimate manly sacrifice and skip the Knicks game to go shopping with you."

"Shopping is a sacrifice?" A look of disbelief was clearly written across her face.

"Real men don't shop."

She looked him up and down. "Those clothes appear in your closet on a regular basis, like magic."

"Something like that." He sent her a wouldn't-you-like-to-know grin, and was mighty pleased to see her blush.

"I don't know, Hennessey. There are some things, like shopping, that are best done alone."

The cab had pulled into an empty space at the curb and stopped.

"Wish you had left your stubborn streak back in Sugar Land, along with your clothes."

Maggie chuckled softly, then stopped as she leaned over John and peered out the window. They were parked in front of a very tall glass building. She frantically looked out all the windows and saw more tall buildings. Not one brownstone in sight. "Mr. Cabdriver." Maggie poked the man on the shoulder. "You're at the wrong place."

"Beckendorf." The driver turned to Hennessey, and said, "Forty dollars, mister."

"This is not our hotel," she stated with absolute surety.

"Forty dollars and tip," the driver yelled, holding out an open hand.

John removed a few bills from his wallet, grabbed his duffel bag and got out. Margaret didn't move.

"Come on, Maggie." He reached back inside and pulled her. Like a rag doll, she slipped out from the back seat of the cab.

"Ohmygod." Margaret stood in front of the Beckendorf and looked up. And up. And up. All the way past the smoggy sky and into the galaxies.

"Let me guess. You're afraid of heights, too."

"Absolutely not." How could he even ask her something like that? "I'm only thinking of our own safety."

"Right." He took her hand and they walked toward the front door. "If I were a gentleman, which I've never claimed to be, even on my best days, I could find us a shorter hotel."

"Fire ladders only go up to the tenth floor," Margaret said in a schoolteacher voice.

When they reached the door held open by the doorman, she ground her feet into the concrete. That horrid, cloying, cold fear once again took over. "Why would Sid lie?"

"Sid always lies." John pulled her through the door. "I'm going to do you a favor," he said, not letting go of her hand. "I'm going to help you get over your fear of heights. Oh, babe, you're going to owe me, big-time, after this trip is over."

"I never said I was afraid of heights," she said haughtily.

She denied any fear the whole time he checked them into the hotel. She continued to deny any fear until they reached the bank of gold elevators.

"Oh no." She backed away. He grabbed her hand and pulled her forward.

"This is an elevator," he said matter-of-factly. "This one is glass, and through the glass you can see the whole hotel. It is run on steel cables, and has guardrails and safety brakes. This elevator is safer than riding in your car at home."

When the elevator door hummed open, Margaret held her head up and marched forward, into the empty glass cage. "I know that."

From the ground floor, Margaret could see everything from the lobby to the guest floors open to the atrium all the way to the glass ceiling. Her throat tightened. She knew when the cage lifted, if she looked out the glass, she'd feel as if she were free-falling.

She did an about-face, intent on heading back out the way she'd come in, but connected with Hennessey's rock-hard chest. His hands held on to her upper arms, stopping her from going forward, keeping her close to him.

"I've got to get out of here." She cringed at the begging in her voice.

"I'll protect you."

No one could protect her. No one. The doors shut. He pressed the button. Forty-five. She slumped.

"Maggie. Look at me."

She obeyed. Oh God. Obeying Hennessey. How had she let this happen?

He lowered his head, slanting his mouth over her lips. He placed his hands on her back and pulled her to him. Her breasts tingled and burned where they came in contact with his solid chest, her nipples hardening to painful, needful peaks. He backed her into the glass wall as the elevator lifted higher and higher. "Close your eyes," he whispered in her mouth. Again she obeyed.

He pressed into her, cradling his erection into her softness, cupping her bottom, pulling her tighter toward him. Her arms reached up, around his shoulders, bringing him down to her. His tongue became a welcome, wanted invasion that she met with longing and hunger. She needed him. He seared her with the rhythm of his body, his mouth, his probing tongue and his stroking hands.

Ping. "Forty-fifth floor," an electronic voice said through invisible speakers. The elevator doors whooshed open.

"Don't look down," Hennessey ordered. "Just keep your eyes on me." He picked up his duffel bag, took her hand and led her out of the glass elevator. "That wasn't too bad, was it?"

She shook her head. Four days. She could almost enjoy her numbing fear for four days as long as he was around to help her forget.

What she couldn't forget was her vision. If the plane hadn't gone down on her way here, then it would on her way back. Four days of Hennessey's kisses and then she'd be dead. Well, at least she'd die happy.

They reached the door marked 4500. Margaret took heart in the fact that apparently Hennessey wasn't as unaffected by their kiss as she would have thought. It was surprising, considering Hennessey's reputation as one of Sugar Land's most sought-after studs. To prove her point, she noticed his hands were a bit shaky as he tried to slip the credit card–size room key into the notch. He hit home on the sixth try.

"This is it, friend," he said as he opened the door and waited for her to precede him.

Margaret's vision wasn't as fogged-up now as it had been earlier. "Where's your room?" she asked.

"Right here."

"I don't think so." She crossed her arms and shook her head.

"There's two rooms and a little kitchen."

"Two rooms or two bedrooms?"

His eyebrow arched and his grin was wickedly sardonic. "Two bedrooms in the bridal suite?"

She turned around slowly. "This is the bridal suite?"

"Yep."

"Did Sid order this?"

After a moment's hesitation, Hennessey nodded.

She narrowed her eyes. "The couch looks big enough for you."

"Maggie. No way."

"The only way."

"What about all those kisses?"

"I'll admit you have a knack for kissing."

"Well?"

"Your technique may have worked when you were in high school, but it doesn't work on me."

"That's 'cause I wasn't in high school long enough to perfect it." He sauntered to the wall-to-wall, floor-to-ceiling windows, and opened the drapes.

Margaret used her hand to fan her face. She didn't think a normal woman could handle a perfected Hennessey.

"Look at the view," he said, letting loose with a long, appreciative whistle.

He had to be kidding. She wasn't getting anywhere near that side of the room. As it was, she could swear she felt the floor sway. Instead she walked toward the bedroom, and a moment later let out her own, more soft, whistle.

"If I have my way," Hennessey called out to her, "this town will be my next home."

"I hope you'll be very happy." Even Hennessey was entitled to his dreams. She stood in the doorway, holding a pillow and blanket. "These are for you. But you've got to see that bed, even though you won't be in it."

He ignored the linen and headed through the bedroom door at full speed, then stopped. Another long whistle escaped through those firm lips. "I've never seen anything like this."

The heart-shaped bed, larger than two kings, took up more than half the room. Fluffy down pillows lined the top. A white lace, goose-down cover, also heart-shaped, draped down the sides and touched the floor. Red heart-shaped pillows of various sizes decorated the head of the bed.

"You know, Maggie, we're friends. Good friends. I can sleep on the right side, you on the left."

She shoved the pillow and blanket into his arms. "That's exactly why you're sleeping on the couch. As a good friend, I feel you should sleep in the room that would be more desirable. The living room is closer to the kitchen."

"Thanks, Maggie."

She smiled sweetly. "That's what friends are for."

Friends. She'd yet to prove a friend to him. Here he really went all out today, taking care of her, making her forget her fears, even offering to go shopping with her, not that she wanted him to do that. He might have been joking when he'd said she owed him. But in her mind, she did. She owed him, big-time.

If she were a real friend, she'd prove it. She'd do something for him that he couldn't do for himself. She helped women in the county escape from abusive relationships, and then start on a career path that gave them much-needed self-confidence. Because of her, they had a chance to start over, to follow their dreams.

She volunteered at the community college, teaching adults to read. By doing so, she gave them a chance to reach their dreams.

She owed it to Hennessey to help him reach his dream, too, if she could. She would make sure that he got his chance to try out for a network anchor spot. She could open doors for him, she knew that. After that, he'd be on his own.

Margaret knew just the person who had it in her power to give Hennessey his dream.

"Hennessey," she said, smiling. "My friend." Holding out her hand, waiting until he put his in hers, she said, "Come with me."

"TOOTIE FRUITY!" Julie Storm ran up to them and gave Margaret a big, bear-size hug.

"I'm glad I caught you while you were still here," Margaret said, stepping an arm's length back and looking at her best friend with a grin that wouldn't stop.

Julie was still as young, vibrant and oh so enthusiastic as they'd both been when they'd graduated from Rice, and both landed jobs at WLS in Chicago.

"I just couldn't believe it was really you on the phone." Julie pinched Maggie's cheek then grabbed her by the shoulders and gave her another hug. "I'm glad you're here."

"Long time no see." Margaret teased. "It's been at least a month since you've been home."

They had been friends since the beginning, when by the luck of the draw, they'd been thrown together as roommates. Julie, now producer of the morning show at the ABC affiliate in New York, was well on her way to the top. Margaret would have been right there with her, neck and neck, if she hadn't had the sudden, all-consuming desire to throw it all in and head back home. The death of her grandfather, the need to stay near the remaining members of her close-knit family had made her reevaluate the direction her life was taking.

"Never thought I'd see you here, friend."

"Well, it's a surprise to me, too."

"You should have let me know you were coming. I would have sent a limo to pick you up. How'd you get here? Train, bus—"

"Plane."

"No kidding! I'll be a son of a gun. Who would have thought it? My little Tootie on a plane after all that happened to you. Miss Indiana Jones and the Temple of Doom and Gloom and all that."

"Maybe my outlook on life is changing," Margaret said. At Julie's skeptical look, and Hennessey's loud guffaw, she protested, "Well, it could!"

"If you were anyone else, I'd say sure," Julie said. "But we're talking about you. And look who you brought with you. Mr. John P. Hennessey in the flesh."

He stuck out his hand. "Nice to see you again."

"You, too," Julie said as she grabbed his hand and shook hard. "So, Toots, are you thinking about moving up to the big time? I've told you before, I'll always have a place for you."

Margaret glanced at Hennessey from under her eyelashes. He had the famous smile on his lips, but it didn't reach his eyes, and his body had tensed. She knew he was thinking it was one more opportunity for her, another loss for him. "I can't leave home," she said. "You know that."

"A girl can always hope, can't she? If I could lure in a prize like you, Tootie, I'd probably get a raise large enough to retire on."

Margaret smiled. "Thanks. If I ever decide to leave, you'll be the first I'll call."

"All right. That's a deal. So, how about a late lunch? That airplane food isn't something I'd feed my dog."

"No, I have some shopping to do before tonight." Hesitating just a fraction, Margaret added very nonchalantly, "Hennessey may want to go."

John recognized an escape attempt when he saw one. Raising one eyebrow at her, he shook his head.

"Let me show you around then." Julie linked her arm with Maggie's and walked toward the anchor desk. John followed behind. This was it. ABC, New York City. The Big Apple. The big time. The difference between this action-packed workhouse and sleepy KSLT was like the difference between a Great Dane and a Chihuahua. The Dane could eat the Chihuahua for dinner. For the first time since he took the job at KSLT, and started dreaming about working in a place just like this, he got that knot of terror in the pit of his stomach.

He felt like a small-town hick. He hadn't realized exactly how big the difference between the ABC affiliate and KSLT was until now. They had four cameras here, instead of one. They had TelePrompTers, and a large crew milling around, drinking coffee, sharing stories. And that was only the part he could see.

The niggling doubt that somehow found him when he least expected it became stronger. What if he didn't have what it took to play in the league with the big boys. Oh, hell. He lifted his shoulders and expanded his chest with pride and confidence. He had what it took. He just needed the chance to prove it. He spotted Maggie and Julie talking in a corner, both looking intense.

As he walked up to them, he heard Julie say, "I told you, Tootie, that it's both of you or just you. But not John alone."

"Since I heard my name, can you tell me what you're talking about?" John asked.

Margaret, cursed with fair skin, felt her face heat, and knew she as turning red. Again. "Okay. Fine," she said. "I'll do it. But under protest. And you know why." She wasn't at all happy with the way things had turned out. She wanted Hennessey to have a chance, on his own, without her.

He had too many points against him in this business. He was so handsome, people didn't take him seriously. They couldn't get past his looks to find out if he had a brain. That's why they wanted the two of them. Station managers considered her the brain and him the bod. And he didn't have a college degree, which may not have mattered if he'd had more experience.

Poor Hennessey. All he had were his dreams.

"What will you do?" Hennessey asked.

Julie grinned at him, pointing the clipboard at his chest. "Johnny, have I got a deal for you. The chance of a lifetime."

She paused, letting the suspense build, making his normally steely nerves turn to jelly. But he knew that if he looked anxious, if he looked desperate, it'd all be over. He crossed his arms over his chest and scrutinized her.

Julie's eyes gleamed back. "Do you believe in fate? Well, I do, and timing is everything. My regular news anchor went on a skiing trip to Colorado. Not only is he snowed in, he broke his foot and has laryngitis. Things couldn't be better for the two of you."

"Really?" He started to smile.

"Oh yeah, things are just great. Tootie's agreed that tomorrow morning the two of you would be the news anchors of my morning show."

"Is this your idea?" He looked at Maggie in amazement. She nodded.

"You did this for me?"

"We're even now. You made me forget my fear of airplanes and elevators. I'm giving you a chance to reach your dream. Remember, though, what you do with the chance is up to you."

"Before you get all sentimental—that's what happens when you live in a small town," Julie cut in. "The deal,

Johnny-boy, is that it's you and Tootie. Not you alone. Got that, hotshot?''

His stomach fell. Nothing had changed. It would always be the two of them. He nodded.

Julie went on, and he did his best to concentrate. "I love Tootie like a sister, but business is business. Anyway, I'm going to start the promos ASAP. You two are hot news right now, getting married and everything."

"You heard about that?" Maggie asked.

"Even the network picked it up. So, Tootie, when's my invitation coming?"

"How about now?" Maggie smiled brightly, and if he knew the smile was fake, Julie surely had to know. "The wedding was such a spur-of-the-moment decision. We'll be getting married on the air, November twenty-seventh."

"The end of sweeps. Whose idea was that?"

John had a new respect for Maggie's friend. If she'd picked up on Sid's plan, probably every other network did, too.

"Can I be a bridesmaid?"

John circled Maggie's waist and drew her close. "That'll be great."

"Fine. I need you both to read for me, and I need to make a test strip. I'll take you to makeup and hair, and you can use the script from this morning's news.

"Will this take long?" Maggie asked. "I have to get to the store. I didn't bring any clothes with me."

"I'll do you first, and then you'll be free to go. Meanwhile, John, why don't you go sit at the anchor desk, and I'll have my assistant run the news through the TelePrompTer for you so you can practice. You'll have about thirty minutes, then I'll have someone bring you to makeup and hair. Deal?"

He couldn't speak, his throat had constricted, so he nodded. This was it. His chance, and Mags—Maggie had given it to him.

He wished Julie had the confidence in him to let him go

it alone, but still, the opportunity was a gift. A precious gift.

Now he had the chance to prove what he'd felt in his gut all along. That he, John Patrick Hennessey, could compete with the big boys. And he'd do it, too. He wouldn't let himself down. And he wouldn't disappoint Maggie.

8

THAT EVENING, Hennessey stepped over the threshold of the bathroom and entered the bridal-suite bedroom. Hot, steamy air and a spicy soapy scent followed him. "What do you think?"

Ohmygod! Margaret took one eye-popping, flash-camera instant photo of him and quickly looked down, but not before getting a good brain imprint of flesh and more flesh. *Think? She was supposed to think?*

Then again, never known for being at a loss for words, she said, "I'll tell you what I think. Ah...well..."

She stared at the wet footprints his bare feet made in the carpet. Feet were innocent thinkable-type sexless objects. If she looked at his feet, all those lusty thoughts every other woman in Texas, and by tomorrow probably New York, too, seemed to have about John Patrick Hennessey would go away. After all, there was nothing sexy about feet.

"Mags? I was only joking. You know, covering up my, uh, invasion of your privacy, having to come out of the shower wearing only this." He tilted his head in the direction of a strategically placed face towel. "There aren't any towels," he added.

"Feet are feet," she mumbled. So what that his were long and perfectly formed size thirteens. She, Margaret O'Brien St. James wasn't turned on. Absolutely not. She had this Hennessey sex-appeal thing licked.

"Mags, I need help."

So did she.

Feet were no good. She looked at his toes instead. Part

of the foot, yes, but safe. Toes were ugly. Uh-oh. Not his toes. Forget that. The flawlessly masculine toes attached to those feet made her heart do flips.

She allowed her gaze to travel along the road of well-defined calves, perfect knees and the most symmetrically perfect thighs anyone had a right to own. Long legs, proportioned, balanced and very lightly dusted with dark, manly hair.

Two pairs of legs. His and hers. Tangled together. Touching, feeling, rubbing.

She sat on the nearest surface. The bed.

"Maggie, go get my duffel bag, will ya?"

And leave this room. Now? No way. Not until she came to terms with all the churning flips her belly was performing.

"Maggie?"

"I'm thinking." Where was she? Oh, yes. His legs. Just because she had a strong desire to run the pad of her foot along his calf, knee and thigh and feel that hair tickle her skin didn't mean she wanted his legs tangled with hers.

"What's there to think about? Geez. Women. Please, Maggie. I'm not decent."

No, they weren't decent—the thoughts she had. Looking at his feet and legs made her mouth go dry. Other, very feminine parts moistened. Very uncomfortable. Very irritating, these reactions to Hennessey. So common. Just like every other woman who saw him.

But she, on the other hand, would overcome the attraction. She was, after all, Margaret O'Brien St. James.

Margaret cleared the strong itchy lump in her throat and slowly, carefully, moved her eyes farther up his body.

And got stuck at the juncture of his legs. Ohmygod. Mountains and peaks rivaling Mount Everest were barely hidden under that face towel. *Move, eyes, move. Now!*

Why in the world wasn't her brain functioning? Not only didn't her eyes find a new place on his body to stare, but every other part of her stopped functioning normally, too.

Hennessey had to know what he was doing to her. No one, not even he, could be that dense.

"I'm a guy, Maggie. If you weren't here, I'd get out of the shower, get my bag and get dressed. But I can't do that now because you're here. And I'd be offending your high-class Victorian women's kind of stuff."

"What?"

"You know. The stuff that gets offended."

"Oh, sure." She nodded. Yes, he could offend her women's stuff. She wanted him to. Maybe if she gave him a hint. Like a smile. One little smile. Maybe a nod toward the bed. How hard could flirting with intent to seduce be?

She didn't want to be a prude. She could be a modern woman. If she tried hard. She'd prove it, too, and make the first move. Surely he'd get her meaning without her having to actually say the words. She twitched her head. Kind of.

He narrowed his eyes, looking slightly confused, and said nothing.

So much for discretion. She flipped her hair over her shoulder, in the direction of the fluffy down pillows. He followed the movement, then brushed his gaze over her, making her skin burn and tingle.

How dare he do this to her?

He stepped closer.

How dare he not? Ohmygod.

That scrap of white material, a facecloth, was the only fabric hiding the male outline of a very masculine Hennessey. She stared openmouthed until he stood directly in front of her, in his might-as-well-just-be-naked glory.

Droplets of water clung to the whorls of hair matted over a Hercules-rugged, tanned chest and reflected in prismlike sparks from the lamp on the nightstand.

Softer dark hair on his head, thick, disheveled, wet and oh so needy of attention beckoned her, *Touch me, touch me.* "I can't," she moaned.

His confused expression quickly turned roguish. "What can't you do?"

A day's growth of dark stubble covered his upper lip and chin. Without the luxury of really touching him, she could almost feel how the bristle on his cheeks would feel on her fingertips.

"You don't know this about me, Hennessey, but I'm weak."

She knew what would happen to her if she ran her lips over his, which she had a deep craving to do. Her chin would become red and chafed from the roughness.

She absolutely had no desire to kiss him anymore. None. Those kisses wouldn't lead anywhere, and she'd only get hurt.

And yet…

Until today, thoughts of the two of them together doing the pucker-lip tango had been so far from her mind, they were almost nonexistent. Two years, eight months and five days of time gone by hadn't prepared her for the barrage of sensations assaulting her now. Could these feelings for Hennessey be a prelude of things to come if she let herself go? What would happen if she really acted upon the urges that her overstimulated imagination had planted in her brain? And she wasn't talking about just kissing, either.

"When you say weak, do you mean you won't be able to lift the duffel bag because it's too heavy?" he asked.

"I can't do it."

"You're being stubborn."

"Not really." She stared at his lips. Bold, firm, strong. Lovely. The thought of kissing him, of their lips dancing together, maybe even singing an aria, had taken on gigantic sensual proportions.

He lifted an eyebrow and cracked a grin. "Get the duffel bag."

She wanted to see more of him. She needed to see everything she had missed so long ago. She wanted to touch him, to feel those muscles and ripples of flesh underneath her fingertips.

She knew she should back away from his nearness, but

since she was sitting on the bed, backing up would only be an open invitation to continue something that had been thwarted months ago.

"Hennessey. Please. Go make yourself decent," she whispered to him, itching to help him become even more indecent, restraining herself from pulling the towel out of his grasp. "Please."

"I will—as soon as I have my clothes."

He hitched the cloth higher on his waist, tantalizing her with a flash of male. His eyes were a gleaming testimony as to how he could read her mind. How wonderful it must be for him to be so confident in his own sex appeal.

"Are there clothes in your duffel bag?" She smiled coyly.

"You know there are." His own grin was just as wicked.

Oh, he had to be kidding. No way would she get that bag for him. She might never get an opportunity to see Hennessey like this again.

"Maggie, look at me."

She *was* looking at him. Just where she wanted to look.

"My face," he barked.

She finally raised her gaze. After all, no point in letting him think she was only interested in his body.

"Mags, it's by the left side of the couch. If it's too heavy, you can drag it."

Was he crazy? "Go get it yourself."

"I don't have anything behind me, if you know what I mean." He glanced down at the face towel.

She didn't hesitate to look back herself. Wow. Even better than before. While the towel may have hidden his male privates, it sure didn't hide his male bulges. If anything, he was outlined and defined. Ohmygod.

She rationalized that she'd had a vision of a plane going down, and her on it. It didn't go down on the way to New York, so that could only mean it was going to crash on her way back home. She had about three and a half days left of life. She might as well use them the best she could and die a happy woman.

Her future demise gave her courage. She swept her hand limply across her perspiring forehead. "I can't possibly help you. I'm weak." Of mind, not spirit.

"Oh, really?" A know-it-all, devastatingly handsome grin broke out on his face as he stepped closer toward her. "Weak women turn me on."

"Stay back," she blurted out, hand extended in front of her as if she could ward off the powerful effect his body had on her. He stopped.

So much for being a red-hot mama ready to take chances before her untimely death. She was nothing but a fraud. She looked at his toes again. They were the safest part. When had those little digits become so intimate?

She willed her spunk to appear again. Mind over matter. Mind over body.

Why shouldn't she stare at him? Why shouldn't she look at the bulge? It's not as if men hadn't been ogling women for thousands, maybe billions of years. If she wanted to give a little special attention to what every other woman in Sugar Land would be dying to give attention to, then she would.

And she did.

"Maggie." Hennessey's strong voice commanded she look at his face.

No way was she changing her view. "I'd love to continue this conversation, but I have to take a shower."

"Need help?"

"No."

"There are still no towels."

"That doesn't matter. I bought a terry robe this afternoon."

"Oh. So, does that mean you want me to leave?"

"Yes."

He gave her that wicked smile again, then looked behind

him for a second, then back at her. That grin should be outlawed.

"Fine." He sauntered toward the door, deliberately tantalizing, giving her every opportunity to see the back half of him, the half not covered.

Ohmygod! *Yes!* She gasped in a gulp of air. She never thought of herself as a butt woman, but hey, who cared what she thought of herself. A butt like Hennessey's could pass for a Michelangelo masterpiece. Not only was his front side perfect, but his perfectly sculpted caboose made her want to whistle and blow smoke.

The door slammed shut behind his *behind* and then he was gone, leaving her with nothing but a parting, "Hope you enjoyed the view," shouted from the other side.

"I did, I did," she groaned in female frustration, leaning back on the mattress, staring at the ceiling. She knew she should get in the shower and get dressed for the dinner tonight. But a moment like this had to be relived a few times in glorious Technicolor. Each strong male muscle, one cute little tush dimple, every part of his body seemed to be tattooed in her memory.

Oh yes, she would relive this moment often in the years to come. But now she had to think about tonight. Would this be the evening Margaret O'Brien St. James threw in the towel? And if she did, would Hennessey be here, or walk out on her as he had done before?

She didn't know if she could take the rejection again.

MARGARET HAD ONE LEG of her panty hose on and one off when the phone rang. Hennessey called through the door that it was her agent.

She lifted the receiver, calling out, "I've got it." After she heard the click of the living-room extension hanging up, she said, "Hello, Bev." She stood next to the nightstand, her panty hose now drooping back to the floor.

"You sound out of breath. What are the two of you doing?" Suspicion laced her words.

"Nothing. He's out there, I'm in here. I'm trying to get ready for that dinner with Fabulous Fat-Free Foods."

"I don't trust Sid."

Margaret laughed. "Who does? So what's up?"

"Are you sitting? I need you sitting for this."

"I'm sitting." Maggie walked to the closet where her dress was hanging.

"Houston's CBS affiliate wants you."

She backtracked to the bed and plopped down. "What?"

"You heard me."

"After all these years?" she asked under her breath. "Why? Why now?"

"Margaret, it happens all the time. KSLT is coming up on their tail, and they want to hire away part of the team responsible for the ratings increase. If they hire you now, they'll have the competitive edge."

"What about my contract?"

"Your contract doesn't have a non-compete clause, and the station is willing to pay KSLT for the remainder of your term."

"I can't believe this," Margaret said, struck by the enormity of the situation. "I've been wanting a job with a Houston station since I moved back to Sugar Land."

Houston and Sugar Land were neighboring cities. Margaret wanted to be near her family, and she took the job in Sugar Land so she could do that. She had turned down jobs that would take her out of the Houston area every week. She refused to leave her family. And now, the position she'd been waiting for had opened for her, and she could hardly believe it had happened.

"Bev? What about Hennessey?"

"Nope. Only you. Just you."

Leave Hennessey? Take a large-market network-affiliate job, that's if she made it back home alive, and not take him along? Yesterday she wouldn't have hesitated.

But that was yesterday.

This was today.

Margaret stared at her reflection in the wall-to-wall mirror. Her teeth worked her bottom lip, chewing. She had been preparing for this moment for what seemed like forever. A job with the network affiliate. Just for her.

Tomorrow morning Hennessey would get his chance to be in the spotlight. The chance he'd been waiting for. He thought that tomorrow would be the day he was discovered.

But she knew the cruel realities of the business.

"Margaret?" Bev called.

"I'm here."

"Why don't I hear the whoop of joy? The bouncing off the ceiling?"

"I can't accept the job." It was the hardest thing she'd ever said. It was also the easiest decision she'd ever made. She couldn't, wouldn't let Hennessey know that she'd been offered the job he'd been dreaming of.

Margaret had to hold the phone away from her ear as Bev screamed, "Are you crazy?"

"You don't understand," she said softly, calmly.

"You're damn right I don't. You know, you just flew in an airplane. I know how that makes you feel. Your mind probably isn't functioning right now. So I'll tell you what I'm gonna do. I'm not going to tell them you said no. I'm going to wait until you get back home, and then you and I will go have lunch, have a few Jack Daniel's—"

"I don't drink."

"Fine. I'll have them. Then we'll talk about this situation rationally. Like grown-ups."

"I'm not going to change my mind."

"Grown-ups without Hennessey hormoneitis."

Margaret let out a deep breath as she hung up the phone. She hoped her decision was the right one.

She slipped on the black dress she'd bought this afternoon, zipped it as high as she could, applied a final coat of lipstick and put the tube inside her new black beaded purse.

Her life had changed since she'd gotten on that airplane this morning.

Hennessey was full of bluster, but inside he was a lot more vulnerable than she was. She couldn't leave him behind. It would be like telling her literacy students they were too old, or too stupid, to learn to read. All they needed was a chance, someone to help them along, to be patient with them. Someone like her.

Someone like her who needed to be needed. Who needed to be loved. To give love. Love. Is that what this was all about? Did she love Hennessey?

Maybe she did. Maybe she always had. Perhaps that's why his rejection two years, eight months and five days ago, had hurt so badly.

Margaret opened the bedroom door and entered the living room. Hennessey stood in front of another one of the many walls in the suite that had been covered with floor-to-ceiling mirrors, roguishly dressed in a black tuxedo. His gaze caught hers and held. His smile, so devastatingly handsome, was for her alone.

"How do I look?" Margaret held her arms out from her sides and turned in a circle.

John wondered if Maggie had any idea how she looked. Did she have a clue as to how she made him feel? No way was she wearing that dress for anyone else to see. In fact, he was calling room service. Screw Sid. Screw Fabulous Fat-Free Foods. As far as he was concerned, they were staying in tonight.

"You can't wear that." No way, no how. The black dress was cut low, her white, creamy breasts were barely contained. The slit up the side showed enough leg, accented by sexy high heels, that he wanted to push the material aside, rip off those panty hose and take her right here, right now.

"It's an original from the collection of the late Versace." Her voice was seductively low.

"I don't care if it's from a discount store."

"Do I look bad?" she asked softly, her words unsure.

"What kind of question is that?" he answered brusquely.

"How does a steak look to a man who hasn't eaten in weeks? How does apple pie look to a man deprived of sweets?"

"That's good then?"

"No."

"But you just said—"

"Forget what I said."

She blew out a shaky breath and smiled.

He drew his eyebrows together. Suspicion and jealousy surfaced like dead fish during red tide. "Who're you trying to impress anyway?"

And they didn't sink with her wouldn't-you-like-to-know smile, even though all she said in a perky voice, was, "No one."

Yeah, right. He was nobody's fool. "Good," he told her. "Because I'm not out to impress anyone who's thinking of cutting out the station's loyal advertisers. Got that?"

Maggie's smile brightened. "I wouldn't, either. I wouldn't even go if I wasn't so hungry. I haven't eaten all day."

John slipped the fallen black spaghetti strap back on her shoulder. When his finger touched her skin, she caught her breath and held it. She looked at him for a moment then glanced into the mirror.

"Hennessey, can you finish zipping me?"

"Geez. How much can a guy take?" He zipped the back of the dress. Her skin, now lavender fragrant and petal soft, burned his fingers. He didn't want to zip the dress up. Every part of him wanted to pull the zipper back down, listen to the teeth grate on each other, watch the clingy material drop from her body and hit the floor. Think *wart. Wart-wart-wart.*

This was bad when wart thoughts did him no good. All he could focus on was how much he wanted to help her step out of the puddle of cloth. He'd carry her naked body to the heart-shaped bed and lay her down, then cover her, warming her with his body.

Here he was in the middle of the most severe case of puppy love he'd ever experienced, and she wasn't even paying attention to him. How could she stand in front of the mirror, smoothing down the black material, twisting from side to side, making her breasts almost explode over the neckline. Why was she purposely torturing him?

For the past three years he'd been so intimidated by Maggie's brain, her intellect, her IQ, her Rice degree, that he'd never given himself a chance to get to know her. Really get to know her. And the one time he'd gotten the chance, he'd walked out on her.

Now he was being bombarded with the beautiful Maggie, the vulnerable Maggie, the compassionate Maggie. The passionate Maggie.

She caught him staring at her. A blush rose from the tops of her breasts, passed her neck and settled in her cheeks. So she wasn't immune to him, either.

"No," she whispered.

"Yes," he mouthed back, lowering his lips to the bend in her neck, tasting sweet skin, tasting Maggie.

Oh, yes, this was good. Real good. He had her just where he wanted her. Let her think of him for a while in the same haunting way he'd been thinking of her. Let her get used to the torturous feeling of unfulfilled desire.

"We have to go now," she moaned. "Or we'll be late."

He stopped kissing her, wiping her skin where his lips had touched with the pad of his thumb, spreading moisture and his scent over the side of her neck. Claiming her.

Now all he had to do was bide his time until they got back from the dinner. No sleeping on the couch for this boy. Hell, no.

9

THE WAY MARGARET looked at it, the first time Hennessey kissed her on the airplane was nothing more than a way for him to make sure she didn't faint from fear.

The first kiss in the Beckendorf elevator had to have been Hennessey's way of saying, "I'll make you forget we're in a glass cage being held by sewing thread."

The second elevator kiss, the one that had happened when she'd finished her shopping and was very grateful he was back from the TV studio and available to escort her up to the suite, came under the Pavlov theory of conditioned response. When she saw a glass elevator, she needed his kiss.

So how could she classify the kiss he'd laid on her as they traveled up thirty stories in the Fabulous Fat-Free Foods building in a regular elevator?

The steel doors had shut. The floor under their feet jerked once. Twice. Then they began to rise in their confined space. Her breathing became heavier, her heart beat faster, her hands became cold and clammy. Hennessey came toward her until she was backed against the elevator wall, feeling the vibrations as the car rose on its steel cable. He pressed his body into hers, his rigid manhood into the softness of her femininity. Her legs became weak as her mind clouded with urgent desire. Then his lips descended upon hers and claimed her.

She stumbled out the elevator on jelly legs. Hennessey held on to her elbow as if to support her, but one glance his way, and then another, more covert peek lower, and she knew for a fact he needed her support as much as she needed his.

Willie had taken an earlier car, and was there to record their arrival.

Margaret reapplied her lipstick with jerky motions then brushed her finger over Hennessey's lips to wipe off the evidence of their kiss.

Willie recorded it all. "Ain't love grand?" he teased.

Margaret started to deny Willie's assumption that they were in love. She couldn't *ever* let Hennessey know her feelings toward him had changed a bit. But before she could say a word, he put his arm around her shoulders, and said softly in her ear, "It's all a game."

Smiling into the camcorder, he said, "Maggie and I are looking forward to getting back to Sugar Land so all the viewers can witness true love in action."

She smiled, too, and hoped her lipstick was on straight. The little more than three days they had left here were make-believe. Their kisses might throw them off-kilter. She may be attracted to him. But in the end, even if she *did* fall in love with Hennessey—which was a pretty sure thing now, she realized—their relationship was only business to him.

How he felt didn't change her earlier decision. She'd done the right thing telling Bev no.

Throughout this whole day, Hennessey had been her knight in shining armor. He had protected her from her fears, watched out for her, made her feel safe and secure. He'd made her feel wanted. Made her think he really liked being around her. That she was special. He'd treated her like a desirable woman, not like the dud she thought herself to be.

Yesterday, if the CBS affiliate had offered her the job, she would have taken it in a heartbeat, and probably rubbed her success in Hennessey's face.

Today, that kind of revenge had lost its appeal.

Hennessey's dream of becoming the next Peter Jennings

meant more to her than taking the affiliate job. There'd be other Houston jobs when she was ready. When Hennessey had found his place.

She hoped.

"Well, look who's finally here." A bone-thin woman, with short, spiked black hair, came over to them, tottering on heels almost as tall as she was. "Our guests of honor."

She included both Margaret and Hennessey in her greeting, but the woman only had eyes for Hennessey.

"I'm Lillith Ridgway, and you must be John." She held out her hand to him, at the same time elbowing Margaret out of the way. Lillith purred, "When Sid said he was sending his top dogs over to schmooze, I didn't expect anyone as pedigreed-looking as you."

Lillith's arm had become a monkey wrench, grabbing Hennessey. He didn't try to disentangle himself. Suddenly, his suit of armor seemed to become a smidgen tarnished.

It's only a game, Margaret reminded herself. She didn't have any claim on him. Not really. What was a kiss? One kiss. Dozens of kisses. What was seeing him in the almost altogether? Nothing. Sort of. Still, there was the issue of the proper way to behave, and New York Lillith, the black widow spider in the red dress, didn't follow the Texas code of conduct.

Margaret put on her St. James smile—the one that said, "I want to kill you slowly so I can watch you die in pain"—held out her hand for a St. James handshake, and with all the Sugar Land charm she possessed, said, "How do you do. I'm Margaret St. James."

It took Lillith a few seconds to refocus her attention on Margaret. Once she did, she held out her hand, too, giving Margaret an overcooked-spaghetti handshake. No backbone that one.

"Margaret." Lillith sniffed the name though her nose, and dropped a few consonants in the process before showing her her back again. "John, your pictures don't do you justice." The spider linked her arm through his and sidled up real close. "Come with me and meet my brother."

"I look forward to that."

"Don't look too forward, darling." Lillith let out an exaggerated breath. "Remember, no matter what Roger offers, you're mine."

Margaret and Willie, left standing alone in the hallway, watched as their hostess and Margaret's supposed fiancé rubbed hips as they walked into the banquet room.

"Were you sayin' something, Margaret?" Willie asked. "I didn't hear you."

"Nothing," she said, clamping her lips.

"You hungry?" Willie asked.

Her growling stomach answered. "I have to eat."

"Way c-o-o-o-l." Willie's normally pallid complexion brightened. "I'll record it."

"Yes. You do that, Willie."

"I'll make it a docudrama called 'Human Waste.'"

She hardly paid attention as she mumbled, "Sounds great."

Hennessey, already in the middle of the banquet room, turned, and waved her in. She didn't move. Watching another woman act stupid around him wasn't her idea of a good time.

He shifted to look at her again, this time in desperation. Ah, much better, she thought, and regally entered the banquet room of Fabulous Fat-Free Foods, with Willie trailing behind her.

No matter what she thought of her hostess, or their reason for being invited here, Fabulous Fat-Free Foods had gone all out for them. The black-and-white art deco banquet room sparkled with silver vellum centerpieces that caught the scattered candlelight.

Margaret had almost reached the twin buffet food tables when Lillith and John tracked her down, dragging a third person with them.

"This is my brother, Roger. Say hi to Margaret, Roger," Lillith ordered.

"Hi." Tall, dark and handsome lifted her hand to his lips. "Ignore Lillith. You know how big sisters are."

Big sister Lillith was half the size of little brother Roger, and right now, Lillith had a leg climbing up Hennessey's.

"I sure do." Margaret nodded toward Lillith's stray body parts. "Know about siblings."

Roger didn't look too pleased and peeled his sister off Hennessey, telling her to behave. "Give a guy a chance," Roger said.

"I saw him first," Lillith hissed.

Roger asked Margaret, "Are you hungry?"

Her stomach answered.

"Come on." He took her arm, but not before sending another look of longing in Hennessey's direction.

Margaret closed her eyes for a brief moment and shook her head. When would the humiliation end? Not only did every available woman in the world want Hennessey, now she had to watch a man go after him, too.

What was wrong with her? Hennessey had said she was steak, but right now she felt more like a piece of raw hamburger.

"Let me feed you the best food you'll ever find in New York," Roger said, handing her a chilled crystal plate.

The tantalizing array of epicurean delights teased her nostrils and sent her starving stomach into spasms of joy. "Everything looks wonderful."

Roger looked over at Hennessey. "Yes, it does. Is he dating anyone?"

"Roger," she said sharply. "We're getting married."

"Pity," came the reply. "Do you know if he'll stray?"

"NO!" As if she knew. Theirs would be a marriage in name only. What hold did she have on him?

Roger took a deep rattling breath. "When we buy KSLT and I move down there, we'll see how strong the brute is."

Margaret would have been fascinated by Roger's batting

eyelashes, if she hadn't heard the words she thought she'd
heard. She tilted her head. "*Buy?* I must have heard you
wrong. Did you say buy KSLT?"

"Of course, darling." He lifted a spoonful of creamy
white fish from a silver platter. "Try the fat-free herring.
It's yummy."

"Can't wait."

He placed a mound on her plate. "Fat-free caviar?"

She nodded. Roger moved up, and when Margaret tried
to follow, she felt something stuck in her side. "Willie!"

"You promised, Margaret. Remember my docudrama."

"My stomach is growling." The camcorder was trained
on her midsection.

"Background noises."

Hennessey's armor began to shine again when he dis-
engaged himself from Lillith's web, grabbed Willie by the
shirt and pulled the cameraman, who protested loudly,
away from her midsection.

Margaret turned back to the food. Food, and an abun-
dance of it, was what she needed right now if Hennessey
was going to have a chance at stardom tomorrow.

The only way he'd get to anchor the news by himself
would be if she was so sick she couldn't go. And she in-
tended to get just that sick.

Never mind that Julie had said it was both of them, or
neither of them. Julie would put Hennessey on by himself
if she had no other choice, and Margaret would make sure
her friend hadn't a choice. After all, ten years of friendship
provided a lot of blackmail material.

That decided, there was one thing left to do, and it
wouldn't be hard because she was starving anyway.
"Roger," she said with enthusiasm. "I've a terrible craving
for those." She pointed to the mounds of perfectly pink
boiled shrimp carelessly cradled within the melting arms of
a Venus de Milo ice sculpture. Her stomach reacted with
joy.

"Beautiful, isn't it?" he asked, not seeming to need an

answer. "I don't know if it was worth five thousand dollars though. What do you think?"

"I'll savor every bite."

"Hennessey." She caught his attention when he returned to the food line. "Try the shrimp. They're priceless."

"I'm not hungry right now." He pinned her with his hot gaze. "For shrimp."

Lillith said, "Let's go find a table and I'll help you work up an appetite."

Roger, with a hand on his hip, looked longingly after the couple. "I'm so jealous. She always gets the good ones."

"She didn't get that one. I'm engaged to him."

"This is New York, darling." He had a mischievous gleam in his eye. "You're not in the provinces anymore."

"I'm not worried." Margaret linked her arm through Roger's, and said, "Now tell me all about this food, and all about you buying KSLT. I want to know everything."

As Roger filled up her plate, he chattered, "You'll love the sardines in thyme-lemon vinegar, mackerel with pineapple and bourbon. Oh, and you'll love this." He used the tongs and speared something from a platter. "Imported all the way from Lake Geneva."

"Switzerland?" Impressive.

"Wisconsin."

"Oh."

"Jumping bullfrog legs. As the French say, 'Slurp it up.'"

"They do?"

"Where've you been, girl?"

"I don't know."

"When we buy KSLT, we're going to turn it into a shopping network for our fat-free food. We'll have on-the-air cooking classes, an on-the-air department store, like a catalog. The station will make us millions."

"Where do we come into this?" Margaret pretended it mattered, but she knew it didn't. As soon as she got back to the hotel, both Sid and Rachel were going to hear from her.

"Oh, darling, you'll be our fat-free spokespeople. That's why we had to see you. To see if you'd qualify. You know, Sid did send us tapes of your broadcasts and you and that Johnny are both so darling. But—" he lowered his voice "—television adds ten pounds. Maybe more. Have some of the semi-fat-free walnut dip for the raw cauliflower."

"Thanks."

Roger took Margaret's elbow and guided her toward the table where Lillith was trying to play footsie with Hennessey. To his credit, Hennessey successfully stepped out of reach.

As soon as Margaret sat down, she felt a foot touching her leg. She looked across the table and saw that potent grin on his lips. The one that made her heart surge. Hennessey's shoe rested next to her chair.

Ohmygod. She picked up the fork and started to shovel the food in, not tasting any of the gourmet items Roger had so carefully described to her.

His foot reached her thigh.

She ate faster.

"Have a glass of champagne," Roger offered, pouring, while still trying to make eye contact with Hennessey.

"Maggie doesn't drink," Hennessey said, never once taking his gaze off her face.

"Just what I needed." She drank quickly, dying of a thirst that couldn't be quenched. Okay, she silently signaled Hennessey. She didn't drink. But then, she normally didn't have his toes making trails up her leg, either. She held up her empty glass. "A touch more, please. To the rim."

His foot reached the juncture between her legs. Conversation went on around her but all she could hear was the roaring in her ears.

Toes stroked parts of her that hadn't been stroked since that night, two years, eight months and five days ago.

"How're you doing, Maggie?" Hennessey's voice seduced her from across the table.

More food went down. More champagne. "Just fine," she managed to say as she speared a barbecue fat-free hot dog. "Fine, fine, fine."

His toes sought then tore through the inner core of her panty hose, reaching up, into her soul. "Ohmygod!" She vibrated from the center of her being to all points outward.

"I knew you'd love that sausage." Roger leaned back in his chair in triumph.

Hennessey nodded. "I can tell by looking at Maggie's face that she's thinking about how to get some of that fat-free sausage home tonight."

Margaret almost gagged.

"As soon as we own KSLT, I'll make you sausage all the time," Roger promised.

"Own?" John's foot hit the floor. "KSLT?"

"I was going to fill you in when we were alone, Hennessey," Margaret said.

"You knew?" He looked at her as if she'd betrayed him.

Her words sounded as if they were coming from another person's body. "Roger just told me." She tried to wink at him, to signal him to be quiet.

His eyelids narrowed, and she'd never seen him look so serious. But he stopped asking questions. He'd put his trust in her.

He came around the table and reached for Margaret's arm while casually covering those incredible toes with his shoe.

"Bye-bye, toes," she mourned.

"Are you all right?"

She looked up at his face and smiled. "I sacrifice so much for you. You'll never know."

"Too much champagne. Come on. Let's get out of here." Holding her up, he walked purposely toward the elevators, ignoring the protests of their hosts. She teetered along as best she could.

He kissed her all the way down the elevator. Her stomach did flips. He kissed her the whole cab ride home. Her stomach rolled. He pressed his body over hers in the glass elevator, making sure she couldn't see anything, only feel. And feel she did, hard muscles, strong legs and arms, lips that stole her breath. He helped her off the elevator. Her stomach churned.

"We have to talk about what Sid is doing, but I don't want to talk about that tonight," he said. "Agreed?"

"Yes."

His hands cupped her cheeks and he looked into her eyes. "I know what I need. Do you need the same thing, Maggie?"

"I need…"

"What, Maggie?" His deep voice was husky, promising. "Tell me what you need."

"I need you to…"

"Anything. I'll do anything." Hennessey's hands were warm, caressing.

"Call 9-1-1." Margaret keeled over, her hands cradled around her stomach as another pain stabbed straight through, even worse than the others had been. All her suspicions were now confirmed. "I've been poisoned."

AT THREE-THIRTY in the morning, John, dressed in a freshly pressed navy suit and his favorite red power tie, sat on the edge of the heart-shaped bed, now a tangled mass of white satin and lace, and watched Maggie sleep.

With each ragged breath she took, he saw his dreams of network stardom wash down the drain. He had hoped, he had prayed that the hotel doctor who had treated her last night had been wrong.

"Food poisoning," the doctor diagnosed.

"Probably the shrimp," Maggie had moaned. "Or the herring, or cauliflower sauce. It couldn't have been the sausage."

Poor Maggie. John twisted a strand of the golden hair

that fanned out on the pillow around his finger. Soft, silky, wildflower fragrant. Maggie. So small, so vulnerable, curled up like a tiny infant burrowed under the pile of bed-covers.

Poor, frustrated John. After the doctor left, it had fallen on him to lay her out on the heart-shaped bed and take off the black dress. He did his best to ignore the painful erec-tion that wouldn't die as he slowly peeled down the panty hose. Maggie, resting on the bed, sick, in pain, was giving him his own version of cardiac arrest as she wriggled around, trying to find comfort.

He had gently helped her into one of her new nightgowns and kissed her forehead as chastely as he could. He heard her murmur, "Only three days left," before she fell into a deep sleep.

That had been over five hours ago. Now, as he stared down at the sleeping woman, he only hoped she'd be able to get up and go to the station. Julie had made it clear that it was him and Maggie together, not him alone.

John brushed her damp hair away from her cheek, and whispered in her ear, "Mags. Maggie. Can you get up?"

"I'm dying," she moaned.

He gently squeezed her shoulders. "You've worked be-fore when you were a lot sicker than this. Remember last New Year's Day? No one would have known you had a temperature of one hundred and four while you were on the air."

"Go away."

He raked his fingers through his hair. "We have to be at the studio in an hour."

Her answer was another long, pitiful, painful moan be-fore she took the pillow and covered her face. Even with her voice muffled, he heard her pitiful cry, "I'm dead."

"You're not dead." His future was. "Can I get you something to eat? Drink?"

Another groan.

"Did I hear you ask for bacon and fried eggs?"

"You're a mean, cruel man."

"You didn't think so yesterday."

"I wasn't sick yesterday. Why didn't you get sick?"

"I didn't eat."

"But Lillith wanted to take a bite out of you."

"Not interested."

"Really?"

"Yes, really."

One dull blue eye peeked at him from under the lace pillowcase. "My tummy hurts," she whimpered.

"Still?"

The pillow over her head bobbed up and down. He pulled it off her face. Poor, poor Maggie. Her skin was red and splotchy. Her pale pink lips were dry and cracked. Sad, bloodshot baby blues stared back at him. "You look like hell," he told her.

"Thank you." She sniffled. "That's better than you telling me to go to hell."

"I wouldn't do that." And he meant it, too. She had tried to help him. It wasn't her fault the food she had eaten was bacteria-ridden. He stuck his hands in his pocket and paced along the side of the bed.

"Hennessey, can you call another doctor? Only this time make sure he's cute, young and single," she croaked out weakly.

He swiveled around midpace to glare at her. His future was on the line and she wanted him to get her a cute, young and single doctor? Was she crazy?

She brought her knees to her chest in the fetal position, and held back the moan he knew she wanted to scream. She was in pain and he knew it. He could see it reflected in her eyes and on the small smile, which wasn't really a smile, trying to cross her lips.

He put his hand on her forehead. Cool and clammy. He replaced his hand with his lips, kissed her gently, and murmured, "The only doctor I would let come near you would be cute and young, Maggie."

The tension around her mouth relaxed.

"But married. He's got to be married. No single guy is going to get to listen to your chest before I do."

"You think so, Hennessey?" She closed her eyes.

Memories of covering her beautiful breasts with the nightgown had him groaning in frustrated agony. "I know so, babe."

He turned to leave the room. It wasn't her fault she was sick. It wasn't her fault Julie wanted both of them. Hell, he had nothing when he'd arrived in New York, and he still had nothing, except three days ahead of him to prove he could be something.

"Hennessey," she called, a weak, soulful sound. "I'm so sorry."

He smiled. "Don't be sorry. Never that." He shut the bedroom door, went into the kitchen and made himself a cup of instant coffee. Taking the cup with him, he returned to the living room and sat on the couch, watching the clock tick away the minutes of his life.

His head snapped around when he heard Maggie shuffle out of the bedroom, her arms wrapped protectively around her stomach.

"What are you doing out of bed?" He jumped up, ready to take her back where she belonged.

"Why are you still here?" she countered.

"The deal called for me and you. A team. Not me alone."

"Julie'll put you on the air. By yourself."

"Listen, my ego's pretty fragile right now, and I really don't think I can take another beating."

Maggie sat on the couch, and patted the cushion, inviting him to sit beside her. When he did, she took his free hand in both of hers, turned it over and traced his lifeline. "I see a man who can do a fine job without me sitting next to him. I see a man who's afraid to try, because if he doesn't try, then he can always say he didn't get the chance."

"Mags, don't do this."

"I see a man who is afraid he'll get the chance and fail."

"I won't fail." His voice was strong and sure.

"You won't know, will you, if you don't go?"

"Julie made it clear," he repeated. "It's me and you. A team. That's the way it always is with me. That's the way it'll always be."

"If you don't go down there right now, you'll go through the rest of your life saying, 'If only I had…' and wondering what would have happened to you if you'd taken the step. If you don't take the chance, you'll never forgive yourself."

He got off the couch and stared down at her. She smiled up at him. A smile of pain, of pride. He bent over and captured her lips and drank in Maggie. Soft and chapped, but tasting like honey to him. "You win. Come on, let me help you back to bed."

"No, go on. Julie said she'd send a limo and it's probably been waiting outside for the last ten minutes. Go ahead. Enjoy it. Savor the hairstylist and the makeup person while you can. I can't wait to see if they can make your ugly mug look really handsome."

He smiled that devilish grin and took several deep breaths. "How can I thank you?"

"Get out of here. And make me proud."

Margaret waited for three full minutes after she'd heard Hennessey get in the elevator before she picked up the phone and called Julie.

"You don't know what I had to go through last night, eating all that horrible food—fish, just to get this sick."

"Oh God, not fish."

"Just so he'd have a chance to go down to the studio by himself."

"But, Tootie, I'd love to give him the opportunity but I'd have to answer to the VP of news. John just doesn't have the credentials."

"How did he do on the strip tape?" Margaret knew he probably did fine. Better than fine.

"The truth was, he did great. You know he sent a résumé tape to me several months ago, and I ran that through the focus group then, and they loved him. He beat out nine others that time. I ran the tape we did yesterday through another focus group, and these folks voted him number one, too."

"Well, then, what's the problem?"

"I told you. No college, and only three years in broadcasting. Not even as a reporter."

"Julie—"

"I wish I could help, but like I said, I have to answer to the higher-ups, too. It's either both of you or neither of you."

Margaret took a deep, painful breath. It was time to let lose the ammunition. "Julie, does your mother know you're living with Michael?"

She was sure that the squeal on the other end could be heard all the way to Texas.

Suddenly Julie's voice returned to gushing professional. "Tootie, look who just arrived. Hi, John! I'll be with you in a sec."

Julie lowered her voice and spoke softly into the phone. "You win, Tootie, but he'd better be good. If he's not, I'll find a way to get even with you."

Margaret hung up the phone with a sigh of relief. Now Hennessey would have his chance. What he did with the opportunity was up to him.

10

MARGARET SAT smack-dab in the middle of the bed, under two down-quilted blankets, her back and head resting against the stack of pillows that were four deep, still feeling slightly sick to her stomach, but extremely pleased that Julie had come through. Just as she knew her friend would.

Now all she had to do was get rid of this tiresome bellyache. The family tradition, for as far back as her mother's side had been named for movie stars, was to treat a sick stomach by counteracting the pain with comfort food.

None of that healthy, fat-free junk that had made her ill last night. And not what doctors normally recommended, either. What she needed was a good, healthy dose of her mama's kind of cooking, which usually consisted of a trip to International House of Pancakes for breakfast, and the candy and ice cream aisle of the grocery store.

Room service at the Beckendorf, those wonderful people, had supplied her with all the comforts of home.

On her left in a neat row starting near her elbow were the M&M's. Near her knee were the hash browns made with onions, cooked in bacon grease, crispy brown on the outside. The plate of well-done bacon was near her right hand.

Normally she would never eat ice cream so early in the morning, but this was a special day. The extra-large bowl of Blue Bell Homemade Vanilla ice cream that her mother had shipped to her had arrived, packed in dry ice, right after Hennessey had left for the TV station.

Margaret thought Blue Bell ice cream was not only comfort food, but healthy, too. There was nothing like ice cream to soothe a tummyache. Especially the way she'd accessorize it.

Room service had also delivered a silver tray that carried little silver bowls filled with special, healthy, comforting ingredients like chocolate syrup, Reese's Pieces, marshmallows, slivered almonds and chopped Texas pecans and, the ultimate for a sick stomach, real whipped cream.

She clicked the remote and surfed through the TV channels until she came to the morning show Hennessey would be anchoring. He'd called her from there, trying to sound nonchalant, acting as if he'd never doubted that Julie would give him the go-ahead. But Margaret heard the excitement in his voice, listened as he ran his words together and felt the same joy for him.

John Patrick Hennessey was about to launch himself off the planet, and only gravity was holding him down.

She leaned back on her pillows, tilting the bowl of ice cream right under her chin so the spoon wouldn't have far to travel. Spoonful after spoonful of soothing Homemade Vanilla made its way down her throat, coating her stomach.

Suddenly the music came on, the credits, the lights, the glitter, and there he was, strutting his stuff, smiling at her— and millions of others.

The ice cream was forgotten. All her self-sacrificing stomach pains took second place to the man staring at her through the small screen with those incredibly sexy, brown eyes. Poised, sophisticated, articulate. Handsome. Charming. Sexy. Wonderful.

If Julie didn't hire him on the spot, she was a fool.

Margaret didn't know she'd been crying until the commercial came on and she looked down in the bowl and saw indentations in the ice cream. Happy tears, she told herself. Hennessey had what it took to make it big.

JOHN SAT across the desk from Julie in her office. The vice president of news lounged in the chair next to him.

He tried to concentrate on the offer they'd made.

"I'll be in contact with your agent Monday morning and we'll start negotiating," Julie told him.

John could only nod. Speech, words, were too much for him. Sure, he told everyone he'd make it someday. That was a bluff. In his heart, he'd always had that little doubt. Now, for the first time since he'd started sending out his tapes, he'd gotten an offer. A job offer that didn't include Maggie. This one was for him, John Patrick Hennessey. Only him.

"You were great today." Julie flipped a ballpoint pen in her hand. "We knew you would be. Had no doubt whatsoever."

The VP crossed one leg over the other, and chewed on an unlit cigar. "Julie gave me the first tapes you sent and I reviewed them a couple of weeks ago. One main reason for not contacting you immediately after the first focus group picked you as the favorite was your lack of credentials."

John nodded.

His soon-to-be new employer continued. "Yesterday we gathered another group and showed them your new tape, and got the same reaction. Can't argue with focus groups, even if your credentials aren't all that we'd like."

John nodded again, starting to feel a little dizzy.

"Do you think Tootie will mind breaking up the act?" Julie asked.

He shook his head. "Maggie's been hoping for news like this." She'd practically thrown him out of the hotel this morning.

After a few minutes of cordial goodbyes and backslapping, the vice president left.

John couldn't wait to leave, too. He wanted to get back to the hotel and tell Maggie the news, to see her face, to kiss her mouth. To kiss her belly button and make her feel all better.

Over the past two days, he'd gotten used to Maggie's

kisses. He liked having her around, and if he wasn't mistaken, she liked being around him, too. Maybe she liked him enough that she'd consider a permanent move to New York. He could drive her up here. They could live together and buy a one-story house in Jersey. That would take care of airplanes and elevators.

"Julie, when you talk to Maggie, don't say anything about this, okay? I want to tell her in my own way."

"Private celebration, huh?" She winked.

"You bet."

"After everything's settled, all the numbers crunched, the *i*'s dotted, *t*'s crossed, we'll all go out and celebrate. In fact, we'll bring Tootie back for your premiere show. We'll call it a 'going out with the old, bringing in the new' celebration."

Minutes later, John left the protected heated building and entered New York City's world of traffic, horns, smog and crowds. His heart raced with the thrill and excitement of the city. Working in New York every day. Being in the center of the universe. This had been his dream for so long, he couldn't believe that right now he was only a signature away from making it a reality.

He belonged here. What he'd worked so long and hard for had finally paid off.

He should be jumping for joy, he should be shouting it in the streets, that he, John Patrick Hennessey, the guy who'd never made it to college, the guy whose high-school teachers had been taking bets on the size of his cell, had fooled them all.

Now came the hard part. How to figure out a way to get Maggie to join him. She could find a job easily. She'd already turned down more jobs in a year than most people are offered in a lifetime.

John moved through the crowds, pulling up the collar of his coat, hardly feeling the nip in the air.

Life without Maggie would be no life. He liked her. A lot. Okay, he liked her more than a lot.

He loved her. There. That wasn't so hard to say, was it? He loved everything about her. Her quirkiness, her kindness, her generosity. He loved her orneriness, her contrariness, her brilliance. He loved the way she looked, the way she smelled, and especially the way she kissed.

He wanted to spend the rest of his life with her, loving her. He wanted to grow old with her, have kids and dogs and cats with her. And he wanted it all to happen in New York City. Or New Jersey, or Connecticut, or any other surrounding state that offered public transportation to his job.

Now he had to convince Maggie to share the dream with him. She liked Sugar Land. She loved being with her family. Convincing her would be a daunting task. He could do it though. Right now he was on top of the world and he could do anything.

He stepped off the curb and into the busy street, pulling open the door of the first cab that stopped for the light.

"Where to, bud?" the driver asked.

"Tiffany's."

"HOW'RE YOU FEELING?" John shrugged off his outer coat and threw it on the chair next to the couch where Maggie sat cross-legged on the sofa.

She was wearing new, crisp blue jeans, and her full breasts were only hinted at under an oversize Yankees sweatshirt. Her face, free of makeup, was still pale, and her golden hair was pulled back in a ponytail. She reminded him of a kid.

Until he focused his attention on her lips. Ripe, full, sensuous. Lips that had branded him forever. Those weren't the lips of any teenager. Maggie was all woman, and he ached with wanting her, needing to taste her.

John sat next to her on the sofa. He toed off his loafers and pulled the coffee table closer to the couch with his stocking foot. Leaning back into the cushions, using the table for a footrest, he took Maggie's hand, soft as he knew her lips were, and held on.

"I'm feeling a lot better. Comfort food helps to settle the stomach," she said.

"Like soft-boiled eggs, dry toast, hot tea?"

"Blue Bell ice cream my mom had delivered, bacon, hash browns with onions. The usual."

He cast her a suspicious glance. "If the doctor hadn't been here to check you out, I'd think you'd staged the whole thing."

"Oh, please." She rolled her eyes. "I'm not that nice. Anyway, Julie let you go on, just the way I knew she would." She grinned like a proud parent whose child has just won his first spelling bee. "You were great, too."

"Thanks."

"You don't sound too cheerful. Weren't they happy with the way the show went?"

"They were very happy."

"Did Julie say they'd call you if there were any openings? Did she take you to meet the boys on the twentieth floor?"

John nodded. "All of that." And more, thought. But he didn't see any point in telling Maggie that the "something" she referred to had come up immediately and had been offered. At least, not yet.

He'd tell her about the job offer in a special way. He wanted to entice her, to convince her to give up her Sugar Land security blanket, leave her family and start her own. She had to move to New York with him. "You know, Maggie, I've been thinking."

"Oh, no. Does that make your brain hurt?"

"Be serious."

"I thought I was."

"Maaaag-geeee," his tone warned.

"Sorry." Her grin said she was anything but.

"All right. Now let's imagine we were both offered jobs in New York? Would you consider moving?"

She cast her eyes down to where their hands were locked. Her throat worked. "I've been offered jobs in many cities over the past couple of years. I've turned them all down."

"Why?"

"I told you before. My parents aren't getting any younger, and I want to be near them. I'm close to my great-grandmother and my grandparents. I know I'm not old, and they're not too terribly old, but still, I need to be near them. It's what makes me happy."

"Do you think they'd want to hold you back?"

"No one's holding me back, Hennessey. I've already done everything I've wanted to do as far as a career. I've traveled all over, had experiences that people only dream about. It's important to me now to stay home, just as much as it's important to you to try and be the next Peter Jennings. Surely you can understand that."

Not really, he thought, more determined than ever to use the famous Hennessey magic to convince her to move with him.

"Hennessey." She glided her fingers along his jaw, staring into his eyes. "We're only on this earth a short time, and I need to spend as much time as I can with my family while they're still here."

"I have family there, too."

"I know you do, and now that I know you better, I'm sure you're close to them, too. For me, though, it's more than that. I've built a life in Sugar Land. There are people who depend on me, and I can't move away and desert them."

He knew she was referring to the women in the shelter and the people she taught to read. She never talked about her volunteer work, and she couldn't possibly know that he knew about it.

"So there's no way you'd move here, or anywhere. You're going to spend the rest of your life in Sugar Land."

She nodded, then cracked a mischievous grin. "But that shouldn't keep you from trying to convince me."

"You can bet I will. I still have three days left in New York."

"I know. And as soon as some brilliant executive comes along and recognizes all that talent you have under that handsome face, you'll have it made. Hennessey, you'll catch your star and you'll be out of Sugar Land so fast, I'll be left eating your dust."

John wrapped his arms around her and pulled her close. "That will never happen, Mag-of-my-heart."

He held on to her, and didn't want to let her go, until he realized his trump card. "Maggie, let's call Sid."

"I tried thirty minutes ago, and he wasn't in yet."

"I'll try again." He walked over to the desk where the speakerphone was and punched in the numbers. "Janice, this is John."

"Oh, John!" the secretary trilled, her girlish sighs filling the room.

Margaret crossed her arms, and listened. Would that sexual magnetism he had ever go away?

"Is Sid there?"

"Yes, he is, but he's getting ready for the big Informational Golf Tournament. The one where the prize is two hundred and fifty thousand dollars."

"Put him on, will you."

"He doesn't want to be disturbed. He's practicing in his office."

"Janice, darlin'…" Hennessey's voice stroked. "He's going to want to talk to me. Just tell him these three letters. F-C-C."

"You mean Federal Communications Commission?"

"That's the one."

While they waited for Sid to come on the phone, Margaret narrowed her eyes suspiciously. "Was that dumb-jock routine you've been putting on all these years some kind of cover? You're not stupid, Hennessey."

"I never said I was, Maggie. You've never gotten to know me well enough to find out what I'm like inside."

He'd never given her a chance to know him. He was the one who'd walked out on her. He was the one who'd made her feel she was lacking. She had known from that moment that she wasn't pretty enough, or feminine enough, or womanly enough to attract a man with the Herculean looks of Hennessey. And that hurt. Too much. "Well, I just—"

"You just thought I was a pretty face— Hey, Sid." Hennessey stopped whatever he was going to say when their boss picked up the line.

"Get me off the damn speakerphone. I'm not talking in any damn echo."

"I can't hear you then, Sid," Margaret said from across the room. "And I want to listen to every word you say."

"You there, too, Margaret? What did I ever do to deserve this?" he moaned. "I'm in a tournament today. You've got three minutes, then I'm hanging up on you."

"Sid, did you think we were stupid?" Margaret asked.

"I never thought that. Gullible maybe."

"Didn't you know we'd find out that you'd put the station up for sale?"

"You know about that?" He wasn't yelling now. His cursing was soft and colorful, and came through the telephone lines with no problem. "How did you find out? Who told you?"

"Last night at dinner. Roger was thrilled about how he was going to turn KSLT into a shopping network."

"That…" Sid's voice rose with every word, then he calmed down.

"Don't call him names. I like him," Margaret snapped.

"I like him just fine, too. He makes a mean soufflé."

"Oh, Sid. I'm so tired of you. I'm tired of the mind games, and the fact that you're selling us out. You can't do this."

"I can and I will. The deal's almost done, and it's too late for you to stop it. You two just continue on your New York adventure, then get your butts back here after you go to see my friends at Cuddle Me Clothing. I want the best price for my station, and the only way to get it is if you raise my ratings to number one.''

Hennessey said in his lazy drawl, ''You know I own stock in KSLT.''

''Who says you do?'' Sid's voice rose to a squeak.

''I get my dividends every quarter.''

''I own stock, too, Sid. And you'll never get away with this.''

Sid added a few more hair-raising words, then said, ''I've already gotten away with it. You'll get married on the twenty-seventh, or you'll never work in this industry again. I'll ruin both of you.''

Margaret glanced at Hennessey. He was smiling. He didn't look concerned, but he may not have realized yet the impact that selling the station, if Sid got away with it, would have on him.

She had a job offer, and she could start work on Monday if she had to. But he didn't. And without the station, unless he had some kind of trade to fall back on, he'd get nowhere in this industry. There was only one Sid. Poor Hennessey.

''Does Rachel know about this?'' Margaret asked.

''Of course she does,'' Sid screamed back.

''He's lying,'' Hennessey said quietly, and Margaret nodded in agreement.

''I've got a golf game to play. I don't have any more time for the two of you. I'll see you in the office on Monday.''

The sound of the phone slamming was loud enough to wipe away the remaining vestiges of Sid's colorful use of the language.

Margaret gnawed at her lip and sighed. ''Well?''

''How's your stomach feeling?''

''Is that all you can say?''

He raised his hands and dropped them. ''What do you want me to say? We're here in New York. He's there in Sugar Land swindling everyone, and heading for a golf tournament.''

"Do you have any plans?"

"Yes. I'm going to call Rachel and warn her. Then I'm going to take you on a tour of the city."

"I mean future plans, Hennessey. What you're going to do if he does get away with this. What are your job prospects?"

"We can worry about that later, okay? Right now, let's have a good time." He dialed nine for an outside line, then redialed KSLT's number.

Margaret waited until Hennessey had Rachel on the phone before she left him, walking into the bedroom. If she hadn't been so sick last night, she would have realized how lonely it had been to sleep alone in that big heart-shaped bed.

She went to the closet and pulled out the emerald green corduroy jumper she'd bought yesterday. Within ten minutes she was dressed. Hennessey had just hung up the phone when she walked into the living room.

"How did it go?"

"Rachel said Sid thinks the papers were filed with the Federal Communications Commission, but they never were. Janice came to work one morning a few months ago and found a bunch of overexposed, or underexposed, photocopies in the garbage can. She took them out to put them in the paper-recycling bin, and realized what she was looking at were photocopies of papers Sid planned on filing with the FCC."

"Thank you, Janice! Thank you, recycling!"

"She's efficient, that's for sure."

"But why weren't they mailed?"

"You know, Sid's basically a lazy guy."

"That's a typical state of being for guys."

"Now, Maggie, be gentle. Don't put me in the same class with Sid. Besides, he worked hard. He had to learn how to use the copy machine all by himself, and you know, for Sid, that's a job. Too bad he didn't learn how to run the postage meter. That was his downfall. He gave the FCC papers to Janice to mail for him.''

''How could she be sure those were the papers he was filing?''

''He didn't bother to lick the envelope. The man has a screw loose.''

''That's debatable. I think he knows exactly what he's doing, but he's so arrogant, he doesn't think he'll get caught. So what did Janice do then?''

''She went to see Rachel, and told her that it was a federal offense to tamper with the mail even if it had no postage on it. So, instead, she put the envelope in the safe behind Rachel's desk, just in case it needed to be mailed eventually.''

Margaret fidgeted with the pocket on her jumper. The soft cotton soothed her hand, and her jumbled insides.

''Give me five minutes to throw on some jeans, and then I'm going to show you a day like you've never had in your life.''

''Sounds good.'' She couldn't wait.

Hennessey stood in front of her, knuckling her chin up so she had to look in his face, at his strong, square jaw, the firm lips that she knew were soft, and into those bedroom brown eyes. ''Smile,'' he said, grinning.

She did her best to return the smile.

''Maggie,'' he said softly. ''This changes everything now.''

She nodded. How could he have known she had been thinking the same thing?

''I don't have a contract at KSLT. There are so many opportunities for me here, more than there ever will be for me in the Houston market.'' He took her hands and held them tightly. ''Maggie, why don't you take one of the jobs that Julie's offered you?''

Margaret pulled her hands from his and searched around for something, anything, until she found what she'd been looking for. With shaky fingers, she dipped into the bowl of M&M's.

"Well, why?"

"I told you why."

"Will you consider it?"

She gazed at him. "No."

"Is that a yes-no, a maybe-no or a no-no?"

"It's a no. No means no."

"Okay. Okay, I'm going to take that as a 'you'll consider it' no."

"Hennessey…"

"I'm going to work on you."

"You can try." She liked the idea of him working on her.

"I'm going to break you down. You know, rumor has it I'm irresistible."

Ah, Hennessey, it wasn't a rumor. It was pure, one-hundred percent fact.

John loved Maggie. He would shout it from the forty-fifth floor of the bridal suite, only he knew if he went near that window, she'd run out of the room screaming.

He had to find a way to convince her to move with him. He knew she could have a job at the same ABC affiliate he would be working for. Julie wanted her. For the first time in three years, the prospect of working side by side with Maggie didn't stick in his craw.

He had earned the anchor position without her. When he entered Tiffany's this afternoon and stood over the cases of engagement rings, his heart had been at peace for the first time in years.

He'd find a way to convince her to share his future. If he had to bring all her relatives to visit them every month, he would. Or better yet, on his new salary, he could afford four new homes in Jersey, and he could move them all here.

Now that he'd solved that in his mind, he went on to counterattack other reasons Maggie would make to stay in Sugar Land. Her fear of heights. He could take care of that easily. Whenever she had to cross a bridge, or enter a tall building, his kissing lips would be right there with her. It would be a sacrifice, having to kiss those full, soft lips of hers, feel her breasts on his chest as he drew her near, to have her legs rubbing his, her soft, womanly parts cradling the erection he knew he'd have.

But, hey, someone had to do it. It might as well be him. He watched her suck the chocolate candies until he couldn't take the pressure anymore. Leaving her in the living room, he went into the other room to change clothes.

His body had been in a constant state of arousal since they'd boarded the plane. He now knew exactly what that mouth of hers could do to him. Tonight, only a few hours away, if everything went according to plan, her lips, her body would be paying as much attention to him as she was to the chocolate.

As they waited for the elevator to take them down, he asked her if there was anyplace special she wanted to see.

"I don't care, as long as it doesn't involve bridges or tall buildings."

"How about a horse and carriage ride in Central Park?"

"That's a great tourist thing to do."

"What I plan to do to you under the blanket is not a 'tourist thing,'" he said, his voice a promise. He was treated to watching her face turn bright red.

She cleared her throat and straightened those slim aristocratic shoulders. "Well…all right…I think that will work." More delicate throat clearing.

"After the ride, we can have lunch at Tavern on the Green."

"What kind of food do they have?"

"Cheesecake."

"For lunch?"

Her blue eyes sparkled, and she rose on tiptoe, placing her face close enough to his to kiss. "Not just cheesecake, Hennessey. How about chocolate-raspberry cheesecake with whipped cream and cherries on top?"

"For lunch?" He was a steak-and-potatoes kind of guy.

"Ooooh." She sighed. "You know something, Hennessey?" Her lips were so near he felt each word enunciated on his mouth as she spoke. "Have you ever kissed a woman after she ate raspberries and whipped cream?"

He gulped. "No."

"Have I got a treat for you."

11

JOHN PULLED the key-card from his wallet. He didn't look at Maggie, he couldn't. They stood in front of the door marked 4500, the bridal suite. Side by side, not touching.

The day had been great. They'd seen New York, and the more he had fallen in love with the city, the more she compared everything to Sugar Land.

He hadn't told her about Julie's offer yet. There had never been a right time, a right place. But he had to make the time soon. Tonight. Because he couldn't stay here without her. If the way he felt at this moment was any indication, he, the Sugar Land stud, had fallen off the deep end into the swimming pool of love.

They weren't even touching. He was just standing next to her, and still he felt all jumbled up inside. Full of yearning.

He had to get a grip, for God's sake. The woman standing next to him was good ol' Mags. The Magpie. That mouthy Mag-o-muffin who had made it her mission to turn his life upside down.

Ah, hell. The woman beside him was Maggie.

Only Maggie. So why was standing next to her in front of a closed door making his palms sweat?

Because he knew it wasn't standing in front of the door that had him going nuts. Imagining what could, what he hoped would take place on the other side of that door made his mouth go dry and his chest tighten.

It had all started with a kiss. One long, passionate kiss in the airplane. Then there were the kisses as they traveled down elevators. More kisses going up elevators. Little baby kisses as they crossed high bridges. Lingering kisses shared in a carriage traveling through Central Park. Hurried kisses stolen between curbs and cabs.

But it was the sweet kisses exchanged with chocolate-raspberry cheesecake on the tongue that about did him in for good.

His fingers shaking, he stabbed the key-card toward the slot at least five times before it finally hit home and the green light came on. Go.

John didn't have to go. He was already a goner.

Whatever would take place between them tonight had been almost three years in the making. Their attraction had simmered beneath the surface, the sexual electricity sparking between them had their ratings soaring. The public had known about the attraction he and Maggie shared, years before either of them had been aware of the magic.

He rubbed the side of his forehead as he held the door open. "Did you have fun today?" He didn't look at her while waiting for her answer. He stared inside the suite. He looked at the ceiling, he gazed at the carpet. He looked everywhere, anywhere, but at her.

She didn't answer and neither did she walk into the suite.

"Did you?" he asked again, as if the question was the most important question in the world.

He silently counted to three before looking down. When he did, he found himself staring into her face, so delicate, so beautiful.

Her cheeks were flushed, and her blue eyes penetrated his soul. Those shaky pink lips that had always put him in a constant state of arousal were now being gnawed raw by her perfect white teeth. He gently laid a finger on her mouth, stopping further destruction.

He heard her quick intake of air, and watched the pulse in her neck beat erratically. Okay, he told himself. This was good. She felt something for him, too.

"Yes." She breathed the word out.

Yes, she had a good time? Or, was this the *yes* he'd been hoping for? Dreaming about? The *yes* yes?

Maggie walked into the living room, and he followed her. The door clicked shut behind them, and finally, they were alone. No more New York crowds. No hotel guests looking up from the lobby into their glass elevator as they kissed their way to the forty-fifth floor. Now it was just the two of them.

She spun and faced him. "We had a lot of fun today, and I know what you want to do now. Oh God. I know what I want to do now." She blew out a frustrated breath of air. "But I have to talk to you."

Talking wasn't what he wanted to do. Maybe it was a female thing. "Sure, let's talk."

He deserved a prize for restraint. He went into the miniature kitchen and brought back two wineglasses and the chilled bottle the hotel had left for them yesterday. He poured, and waited until she had settled into the couch before he handed her a glass and sat down next to her.

"You don't have a contract," she stated matter-of-factly.

He scowled at her. Not only was that the most unromantic subject, it was a sore point with him, too. He took a couple of swift gulps of wine, then put the glass down on the coffee table. "Is there a point to that remark?" Was she trying to ruin the mood?

"I've always been a tiny bit jealous that you didn't have to have a contract and I did. You always had the independence to pick up and leave if you wanted. That luxury, that freedom is something I don't have."

He ran his fingers jerkily through his hair and tried hard not to snap at her. The whole thing with Sid and contracts was still a raw subject. Even if the way he'd been treated by Sid didn't matter anymore, the lack of confidence Sid had had in him was like a festering wound.

"That's rich, Maggie. Only you would think having job security and a boss who has confidence in your ability would be a crutch."

"Sid has confidence in you."

He faced her, grabbed her by the shoulders and wanted to shake some sense into her. To make her understand. "You think *not* having a contract means your boss has confidence? You think it means freedom?" John worked hard to keep his voice controlled, to stop the tormented feelings from surfacing. Not easy when his insides were knotted.

Her eyebrows were furrowed, her expression one of guileless innocence. She was a woman who, despite her run-ins with every kind of mishap, still had it all.

"Not being offered a contract is Sid's way of telling the world that he can dump me when someone more suitable, more educated, better-looking, whatever, comes along. It's not having job security because the bossman says I'm replaceable. It's knowing no matter how good I am, how much I bring up the ratings, how I struggle twice as hard to get what you're able to get just by breathing…" He paused and took a deep breath. "It's just never going to be good enough."

She started to shake her head but he wouldn't let her get away with that.

"Not having a contract means I have to prove every day, every hour that I'm better than anyone else. That I'm worth more."

"Why have you stayed at KSLT? Why haven't you looked for another job?"

"You don't think I have?"

She shrugged. "I don't know. Remember, you and I have had little to do with each other these past couple of years."

"Right. I don't wear my failures on my shirt pocket, like some kind of badge."

"I don't understand."

"Why should you? Everything has been easy for you, Maggie. Your agent whispers to someone in a crowded, noisy restaurant that the award-winning Margaret St. James wants a job, and the industry jumps."

She had the good grace to at least blush, and gave him enough respect not to try to deny the truth.

"I'm sure if you tried a little harder to let people know you were interested, they'd be falling in line to hire you."

He gently chucked her under the chin. "I never thought of you as being *that* naive." He continued to rub the baby-soft skin under her chin, down her neck.

"I'm not naive," she said huffily, pushing his hand away. "And you haven't tried."

His laugh was full of irony. "I hate to burst your bubble, but the fact is, ever since our ratings started to climb over a year ago, my agent's been sending out my résumé tapes everywhere. I would have taken a lower salary in any of the top ten markets—"

"Really?"

"Nah. I couldn't live on less than Sid's poverty-level salary." His thumbs made small circles on the back of her neck.

She took a deep breath and nestled closer to him.

"Luckily, I didn't have to sell myself cheap. No one wanted me without you. I'm nothing but a high-school dropout, making a living at a third-rate station, even if that station is currently number two in the Houston market."

"You have a lot to be proud of, Hennessey. Bringing up the ratings like we've done is something very few stations have been able to do in such a short time."

"Right. But if you hadn't been there to badger the hell out of me on the air, I'd still be doing sports."

"I'm sorry things have been hard for you. I wish I could help make it better. I had thought after watching you this morning—"

"Hey, we can talk about this morning later." The Tiffany box was burning a hole in his pocket.

"Okay. But we will talk about your future. We will figure out a way."

"Maggie, Maggie, Maggie." He wrapped his arms tighter around her, bringing her closer to him, resting his chin on the top of her head, breathing in the aroma of her wildflower shampoo and the scent of Maggie. "What are we going to do?"

What was he going to do with his reaction to her? Her breasts cushioned against his chest, her warm breath tickled his throat, heating his already overheated body. She didn't make things easy. "You always know how to keep me humble."

"I don't think so." Her denial was muffled in his chest.

"Yes, you do. But things are changing now."

"Nothing's changed, Hennessey. Not really."

"I owe you a lot."

"I know." She twiddled with his shirt button.

"So modest." His laughter rumbled against her cheek.

"Modesty has always been one of my strongest qualities." She winked up at him, tweaking his chest though the shirt.

"And tenacity is mine."

"I admire that about you." She pulled away from him, picked up the wine and took a sip, then looked him straight in the face.

"I'm a jerk." His fingers reached into her hair, caressing golden silk. He closed his eyes, feeling, wanting.

"I want to ask you something else." She laid her head on his chest, rubbing the material of his shirt between her fingers, holding the glass in her other hand. "Two years, eight months and now six days ago, you walked out on me. Why?"

"I was terrified." Without letting go of her, he stood, while two fingers tilted her head back so he could look in her eyes.

"Of me?" Her blue eyes widened in surprise. "Me?"

"Yes, you. Miss Perfect. Miss 'I've got everything.' I was terrified I wasn't good enough. That you'd reject me. That you'd tell me I'd always be a nobody."

Tears pooled in her baby blues. "I would never have

done that, Hennessey. You made me feel like I was a failure at womanhood.''

He used the pad of his thumb to wipe her tears, and his lips to kiss the hurts goodbye. ''I told you I was a jerk. I can't turn back the clock. If I could I would take those memories away. Believe me when I tell you—'' his voice was low, husky and seductive ''—you've never been a failure at womanhood. Your womanhood has been making me act like a randy schoolboy since the first day I saw you.''

''Really?'' She breathed the word out as she unbuttoned the top button on his shirt, running her finger between the next button and his neck, burning his skin with her touch. ''Well, now I need to see if I can make you act like a randy man. You can tell me if I pass or fail.'' The second button went.

''Pass?''

''Or fail.'' The third button was history. Her fingers caressed his skin, his heart skipped beats beneath her touch.

''You're a special woman.'' He lowered his head, pressing his lips to the curve of her neck, finding happiness in her fragrant warmth.

She tilted back, giving him access. ''Do you mean that?''

''I'm an honest man, Maggie. I've never had a reason not to be.''

She moaned with each nip, each lick. ''You've always been special.'' He cupped her buttocks, bringing her soft, womanly parts closer to his hardness. ''More than you'll ever know.''

Even through their clothes he could feel every curve, every indentation. The quickness of her breathing matched his. He slid his hands down the side of her ribs to the indentation of her waist. He reached the zipper on the back of her jumper and pulled the small tab down. The rasp of metal was the only sound in the room.

She let out her breath as the green material slid down her body and pooled at her feet. ''This is the end of something, isn't it?'' she questioned.

He gazed into her eyes and what he saw reflected in the liquid blue pools threw him for a loop. Maggie, so intense, yearning, seeking. He swallowed hard. "Yes. It's the end."

She nodded.

"It's also the beginning."

He extended his arm and held his breath, waiting until she accepted the inevitable. Not until she grasped his hand did he allow himself to breathe again.

After all this time, the two of them would finally come together as one.

Two years, five months and six days had passed since the last time she and Hennessey had been alone together in a bedroom. Only this time they would make love, she was sure of that. Just as she was sure things between the two of them would no longer ever be the same.

And for that she was grateful.

The first time they'd almost made love, so long ago, John had been the one to lead her into the bedroom. Tonight it would be her turn to lead the way, and the idea of taking him in hand excited her.

Tonight she would prove to him that it didn't matter if he worked at KSLT the rest of his life. All that mattered was that they were together. That he was happy, and that he knew he was loved.

"I could play coquettish, or hard to get, but I don't want to waste time." She undid his jeans and pushed them down his legs, then slipped her fingers inside the waistband of his boxers, but explored no farther. She felt the muscles in his abdomen contract and heard him inhale a deep ragged breath.

"Maggie." He covered her hand with his. "I've never told anyone this, but I'm telling you. I love you. And when we make love, it's for always, not only tonight."

"All right. Always." She shyly smiled at him.

His lips formed a grim line. "Well?"

"What?"

"What about you?"

"I love you, too, Hennessey. I wouldn't be here with you if I didn't."

His lips relaxed, and his eyes sparked with desire.

She moved away from him and slowly unbuttoned her blouse, watching his brown eyes smolder as it fell down her arms and dropped to the carpet. She reached behind her, unsnapping her bra, but waited a fraction of a second too long, because he reached out and pulled the lace from her hands, releasing her breasts to his hungry gaze.

She moved next to him and leaned into him, the tips of her breasts rasping over his chest. She sighed deeply, her nipples hardening against him, yearning for his touch.

She cradled his rigid manhood against the yearning center of her core, and rubbed him with her body. They didn't speak, they only touched, until she backed away from him, her legs and arms weak with desire and painful yearning.

He didn't let her get too far away. He pulled her back, and kneaded her creamy flesh, his hands cupping, stroking, circling. His mouth covered her pink nipple and lavished it with attention.

She moved her hips near to him. She turned the hand she had placed in his waistband so now her palm rested against the iron muscles of his abdomen, her fingertips heated by his skin. Her eyes closed and she savored the feel of him.

As he stroked her arms, shivers of desire cascaded throughout her body. His hands created a pattern of gentle caresses down her ribs, his mouth following close behind. He took the tip of her breast and suckled, laving her, sending a wave of desire straight to her center.

Hands roamed to her back, kneading, relaxing tense muscles, accelerating her breathing. How did he do that? How did he make her legs turn to jelly at the same time he made her stomach tighten with unfulfilled need?

"I don't want you to think I'm fast." But she *did* want him fast—and hard. "But I've been waiting a long time."

His voice was whiskey smooth with desire. "I don't want to wait any longer."

She caressed the springy soft hair surrounding his navel, leading a path downward. She ran her fingers down the path, teasing, feeling, until she felt his soft tip.

"Maggie." He groaned out her name, as she bit back her own need. Touching him, being this close to him, breathing in the scent that was male and Hennessey, was as tantalizingly close to heaven as she was likely to get on earth.

He stood over a foot taller than her. If she tipped her head up just a little, her mouth reached his neck. If she stood on tiptoe, her mouth could drink from his.

She opted for the mouth. Just as her toes balanced her weight and her lips took aim, his strong arms lifted her off her feet, carried her to the lacy quilt and gently laid her down on the bed.

"This is my fantasy," she murmured. "You're my slave."

"Do with me what you will." He placed one knee on the bed, next to her hip. With a cockeyed grin on his lips and seduction in his eyes, he said, "Who am I to stop you?"

She placed the palm of her hand over his erection, still covered by his red silk boxers. Her breath lodged in her throat. She closed her eyes, not wanting to see, only wanting to feel. She slid her hand down the length of him. He was ready for her, hard, rigid and vibrating.

She slipped her hand inside the waistband, and slowly, painstakingly, lowered her fingers inside, teasing the length of him, palming him, feeling the power of his wanting her, as her hand captured the very essence that made him a man.

She wanted to savor him, imagine him completely naked. She knew that soon, very soon, what had been two years, eight months and six days in the making would become her reality.

"Maggie," he moaned. "Look at me."

She shook her head. She couldn't.

"I want to see your eyes."

Slowly she raised her gaze to meet his, wanting to give him what he needed. He'd asked for so little, really. Only to have a chance to be like Peter Jennings. She'd tried to help him reach his dream, she really had, and she'd failed.

She wouldn't fail at this.

He'd given her so much. His protection, his faith in her and understanding. She saw in his eyes, the mirror to his heart, heat, passion, lust and hunger.

She saw in their depths the one emotion she had hoped to see, but in the back of her mind never thought she would. Love.

Her hands bunched the red silk and slowly slid it down his hips.

She glanced down. Ohmygod. A whoosh of air left her lungs, and when she tried to breathe, something caught in her throat.

"What do you think?"

She sat up, placed a hand on his shoulder and pushed him down on the bed, taking the lead, giving him back all he'd given her.

She went for his lips, wanting to drink in the taste of him, pressing her tongue into his mouth, meeting his, matching his, brushing, circling, then sipping what he had to offer.

"Oh yeah," he said when she broke contact. "Push me over, push me down, take me."

Climbing on top of him and straddling him, she said, "I'll push you, all right."

Slowly, tantalizingly, she continued to unbutton the shirt he still wore. With every button undone, her lips met Texas-tanned skin, the kind of tan he would never get in New York. She placed long, slow, lingering kisses on each rib and was rewarded when he reached up and laved first one breast then the other.

She kissed his brown areolas, then nibbled her way down

his abdomen, her breasts rubbing skin, arousing her, arousing him, as she followed the path home.

Every kiss brought a moan, and each moan brought her joy. Finally, after all these years, she could touch him, feel him, know him. She wanted to give him as much frustration as he had given her all these years. She wanted to finish what they had once started.

Her hand circled his hard, swollen sex, stroking him down, stroking him up. With every touch he leaned deeper into her hand, his breathing quicker, his own hands fervent in their return caresses.

Each of his strokes followed her rhythm. Palm and fingers sliding slowly down her abdomen, cupping her mound, two fingers stroking her moist core, probing inside in rhythm with his tongue and mouth laving her breasts.

She brought his hard sex to her center, teasing the sensitive silken tip with hot womanly lava. He writhed beneath her, pressing himself harder, grabbing her by the shoulders and bringing her head down to his lips, devouring her mouth with his tongue, matching stroke for stroke what she did to him below the waist.

She squeezed his length, and could feel his life blood pumping inside him. She lifted her hips, guiding his sex to her opening, bringing him inside her, slowly, then pulling out again.

He said, moaning inside her mouth, "You're driving me crazy," and without skipping a beat, continued to feed upon her lips and tongue. Her heart echoed his sentiment.

She lowered herself onto his sex, filled herself with him, clenched her muscles around him, and didn't want to ever let him go. This was Hennessey, the man she had fought with, dueled with, the man who had protected her, watched out for her, stood by her. This was the man she had fantasized about. The man she wanted. The man she needed. The man she loved.

His hands journeyed to her hips, sliding her up on his erection, pushing her back down again. She followed the rhythm he needed, the rhythm she wanted. He incited her, inflamed her, burned her with passion.

His hands cupped her breasts, massaging, palpating the fullness of her. He turned his mouth to her nipples rigid and needy.

With each pull of his mouth, each downward stroke on his sex brought her closer and closer to the crest.

"Hennessey," she called out to him, her fingers grasping the muscles in his shoulders for support.

"I'm with you, Maggie." He lifted her higher, pushed deeper inside her, giving and taking in equal measure.

His touch inflamed her, their passion fueled her need. He didn't stop his caresses, his slow stroking massage a contrast to the quickening of their joining.

She heard his moan, heard him calling her name and with one swift downward spiral, she found her release.

John turned her over on her back and still deep inside her, he slowly branded her with his kisses, leaving no part of her fevered body untouched.

His heart, beating against hers, slowed. "I can get used to this," he said, pulling the quilt over them.

"Me, too," she admitted, wrapping her arms around his back, closing her eyes, giving way to exhaustion and contentment.

"You know, Maggie, we never would have gotten to know each other this well—" he kissed her earlobe, moved down her neck and rested at her shoulder "—if we hadn't gone to New York."

"I'll be sure to thank Sid in the morning." She closed her eyes, letting her muscles relax, giving herself over to exhaustion. "If he's not in jail."

John stroked Maggie's cheek, pushing strands of golden hair off her face. He cradled her, massaging her back until he heard her deep even breathing. She was beautiful and passionate. And he knew this night had meant as much to her as it had to him.

"We'll have a lot to talk about in the morning," he promised a sleeping Maggie.

He slipped out of bed and went into the other room. Pulling his wallet from the pocket of his discarded jeans, he searched for Julie's business card.

Taking a few sips of the half-full glass of wine still on the coffee table, he dialed Julie's home phone number, and waited patiently until she answered.

12

MAGGIE RUBBED sleep from her eye and grabbed for the screeching phone before the third ring. "'lo."

"Tootie!" Julie barked into her ear. "Wake up!"

"I'm up." She had one arm and one leg tangled above the quilt, and one eye opened, looking at the empty side of the bed where Hennessey had lain.

"What time is it?" Julie asked.

Margaret had to clear her throat a few times to get rid of the gravel. "Morning. I think."

"Good. You're coherent. Do you realize what you've done?"

She and Julie were best friends, and they had few secrets. However, some things—like what had happened last night between her and Hennessey—were sacred.

"Tootie!"

"Why are you shouting at me?"

"I'm coming over."

"That's not a good idea right now." Not when she was lying in bed naked and making plans to spend the rest of the day in the same state. She was pretty sure Hennessey could be convinced to go along with the plan. "Tomorrow maybe? You can meet us at the train station."

"Do you have any idea what happened last night?"

"Ah, well…the question should be, do you?" It was too early in the morning for this. She needed six cups of coffee before she could think, and Julie, the morning witch, knew that. "Is that a rhetorical question?"

"Where's John?" Julie asked.

"If I remember, and I was half-asleep when he told me this, I think he said something about going down to the corner and bringing back croissants and coffee."

"Are you sure?"

"I think so. You know I need coffee in the morning. Why? Did you want to come over for breakfast?"

"I want to—"

"Before you say yes or no, I think you should know I'm only asking you out of politeness, because even though I love you, I don't want to see you today."

"Really?"

"Well, you know how it is, Jules," Margaret whispered.

"Then you're alone now, right?"

"I think so. Hold on a second." She covered the mouthpiece and yelled out Hennessey's name a few times. She listened, but didn't hear any answering response, any rustling from the kitchen, or water running in the bathroom. "I'm alone."

"Tootie, did John talk to you yesterday about what happened at the studio?"

"N-o-o-o-o." The thought that something had gone terribly wrong when he was there without her to guide him slammed her in the gut. If there had been a disaster, it would be all her fault. Julie hadn't wanted him to go on by himself, but Margaret hadn't given her a choice. She made sure when she answered her friend none of the worry was evident in her voice. "He came back in a good mood, and said you were happy with his performance. You were happy, right?"

"Yes. Very happy."

Margaret breathed a sigh of relief. Of course she knew Hennessey could do it, she told herself. She had seen him herself on TV and he had been great. "Well, as long as things went okay, I'm glad. Tell me, have you bought your plane ticket for the wedding yet?"

"I wanted to talk to you about something first. About the job we offered John yesterday."

"A job?" she asked, stunned.

"We want him to anchor the morning news. We were in the process of working out the details with his agent. He'd accepted, said he was going back to the hotel to tell you the good news. We shook on the deal and I thought everything was all right."

"He never told me." Maybe he'd tried, and she'd never given him a chance. All those questions about if she'd move to New York. She'd been so busy feeling sorry for him, it had never occurred to her that he'd been hiding news like this from her.

"Then last night, around midnight, he called me at home, and declined the offer."

"Why would he do that?" Margaret whispered.

"I'll tell you why, Tootie. The guy is nuts in love with you, and he said you won't leave Sugar Land. And he won't leave you."

"He gave up the job because of me?" Her stomach tightened. Her head began to whirl.

She couldn't let him make that sacrifice for her. Somehow she had to convince him to follow his dream. He couldn't give up everything because of her. She sat up, fully awake now. The quilt fell to her waist, exposing her naked breasts. Her nipples tightened in the cool air, and she sank back under the covers, warming herself. "Julie. I'll talk to him, and I'm sure he'll see reason and get himself back on track." Margaret hung up the phone, climbed out of bed, threw on the gossamer robe she'd bought along with the terry one yesterday, and went into the living room to wait for him.

The telephone rang again, just as she heard him put the key-card in the door.

The first sight John saw when he opened the door to the suite was Maggie standing in front of the window, the window she'd made it a point to avoid, wearing a filmy white robe that revealed, more than concealed, her nakedness. His body immediately tightened.

She held the telephone receiver in her hand and was listening intently to the person on the other end. Her body, flush, pink, smooth, teased him, hardened him with want and need. He had a craving for her so deep he didn't know if he'd ever get his fill. The more he'd had of Maggie, the more he wanted.

He dropped the bag of pastries on the table, and placed the plastic cups of coffee on the counter. To hell with this frustration. "Hang up the phone," he whispered loudly in her ear. "Let's go back to bed."

Her head jerked side to side.

He'd been so busy admiring her body, he'd failed to notice the stricken expression on her face. "What's wrong?"

"Rachel, hold on, Hennessey's here. Let me tell him the news." She listened to the voice on the other end, then said, "Sid made a hole in one."

"Great. Knowing Sid, he cheated." He took the phone from Maggie. "Bye, Rachel."

"Don't hang up," came the scream through the phone.

"Come on, Rach. Give a guy a break. Now that Sid's happy, I want to take Maggie into the other room and make us happy. Fair is fair."

He gave Maggie back the phone and immediately began to nuzzle her neck. He loved her scent, her softness. The rounded spheres of her breasts, the dusky tips, the light blond triangle at the juncture of her thighs that made his jeans feel too tight. "Hang up."

"Rachel," Maggie said. "I'm putting you on the speakerphone."

John groaned. "Come on, Maggie. We'll see her in a couple of days."

"I have to talk to both of you," Rachel said. "You need to get on the next plane back to Sugar Land. I need you both here immediately."

"No!" Maggie said. "I was going to take a train."

"Absolutely not. I have things to do."

"Listen to me. Sid played in that golf tournament yesterday. And he made that hole in one. But the strangest thing happened. The ball popped back out again. There it sunk, and there it popped. Sid about had a fit. According to what the other people there saw, he clutched his chest and started screaming."

"That's like Sid, all right," John said.

"But then he stopped, and fell on the green. Dead."

"Dead?" they both said at once.

"Dead."

MARGARET AND HENNESSEY sat next to each other in the bulkhead as the airplane headed south. Willie's seat was all the way in the back this time, and she was grateful that her humiliating fear wouldn't be fodder for Sugar Land news.

Hennessey did his part, kissing her breathless under the gray airline blanket all the way down the runway, all the way up to thirty-two thousand feet. Then he had to come up for air.

They had left New York so fast, she didn't have a chance to talk to him about the job he'd been offered at the ABC affiliate. But now he was a captive audience and she had to do what she had to do. Painful as it would seem to both of them. She couldn't let him throw away his life.

"I can't believe Sid's dead." He shook his head slowly.

"I can," she answered. "He was a wicked man."

"He gave me my first broadcasting job."

"He gave you your *only* broadcasting job." She watched his reaction, but he didn't bite. He didn't tell her he'd been offered his pie in the sky.

"Rachel ran the station anyway," Margaret said. "It's not like things are going to be too different. Except about us getting married."

His head shot up, and he stared at her. "What do you mean?"

"You know how I've felt about the whole situation from the beginning. It's unethical. I'm not going to marry you on the air. Sid was absolutely out of line when he came up with that stupid scheme.''

"Marrying me is a stupid scheme.'' Hennessey's tone was both incredulous and hurt.

"Not only that, but, well…with Sid gone, I feel like I need to make a change, too.''

His eyes narrowed. "What do you mean, change?''

This was the hardest thing Margaret had ever done. But she loved him. She had no choice. Holding her perfectly manicured fingers out in front of her, and pretending to admire the red tips, she said, "The CBS affiliate in Houston offered me the anchor job of the six and ten o'clock news. It's just what I've been waiting for. Now I can stay in the Houston market, be near my family and have the job I've dreamed of for the past five years.''

He crossed his arms over his broad chest. She wished those arms were around her.

"Are you taking it?'' he demanded.

"Hennessey, it's what I've always wanted. Of course, I'll be sorry I won't be working with you anymore. I'll miss you.'' She couldn't help the sentimental smile and the sadness she knew was in her eyes at the thought of not being around him every day. But she could only act so much before the raw reality of losing him began to set in. "But a girl's got to do what a girl's got to do.''

He frowned at her. His breathing came quicker and she knew he was angry. If she didn't love him so much, she wouldn't care whether or not he took the New York job.

But she did love him, and because of that love she had to push him north. She couldn't let him give up the one thing in his life he had worked for, sacrificed for, just because they had fallen in love. That would be horrible.

"You're taking the job.'' It was more a statement than a question.

She nodded.

"A job just for you, not the two of us?''

Her nods were quicker this time.

She kept telling herself that she was doing this for his own good. Someday he would be thanking her.

She lifted the window shade, glanced out at the clouds, felt her breakfast creep up to her throat and lowered the shade. She stared at the wall of the bulkhead instead.

She heard the seat belt next to her unsnap, and that brought her attention right back to Hennessey. "Where're you going?" she asked, her voice bordering on panicky.

"Back with Willie."

"You can't leave me alone." She grabbed his arm.

He shrugged her off. "Oh, babe, you're already alone. Enjoy your lonely life."

MARGARET AND HENNESSEY held up opposite walls in Rachel's office. The rest of the KSLT staff were milling around, laughing, talking, drinking coffee and tea, and consuming major fat grams on doughnuts and assorted pastries. Rachel sat on the edge of her desk and called the meeting to order.

"Take a seat, everyone. If there aren't enough chairs, find a place on the carpet."

Margaret was just grateful that her vision of the airplane going down had been wrong. But she wouldn't test fate a second time. She'd tried to explain that to Essie, but her sister, the twerp, refused to hand back her jewelery.

She wished everyone would take their seats so they could get this meeting over with. "Hurry up," she snapped at her co-workers, glaring at Hennessey.

"'Hurry up' wasn't in your vocabulary last week," he taunted from his side of the room.

"Now, now, children," Rachel said. "Margaret, will you pass out these boxes of golf balls, please?"

Pushing herself off the wall, Margaret grabbed a stack of balls with Sid's dearly departed face imprinted on the top, and handed them to the person nearest her. "Take one, pass them down," she said, taking a second stack and giving the same instructions to the man sitting on the other side.

"Do you know what you all are holding?" Rachel asked after everyone had a box.

"Sid's balls," Margaret answered in disgust.

"Sid's dearly departed balls," Chen Ho corrected.

"Is this a commemorative gift?" Stephanie called out.

"Are these worth any more now that he's dead?" Janice asked.

Rachel smiled benevolently at all of them. "You're worth more now that Sid's gone on to the great golf course in the sky." She picked up a file folder and pulled out a stack of papers. "You know, I've been a naughty, naughty girl."

Margaret stared wide-eyed at Rachel. The woman had giggled. Rachel, the number-one number-crunching little mouse had come alive. When had that happened? She looked skeptically over at Hennessey, and saw that he was wearing a similar look of disbelief.

"Well," Rachel began. "I think of all of you in this room like family. I've never understood why my stepfather willed forty-nine percent of KSLT to Sid. I've finally figured out that it had to have been some kind of guy thing, because my stepfather certainly knew Sid wasn't worth two percent, let alone forty-nine percent.

"I was the one who'd worked here all my life and I knew the ins and outs of this business and could crunch numbers like no one else. Fortunately for all of us in this room, the only numbers that Sid could crunch were his golf scores, as those of you who played with him can testify."

There were murmurs of agreement from the staff.

"So, my co-workers, it fell upon me as chief financial officer to set to rights the situation that Sid was so apt to try and ruin. Sid, may he rest in peace and never descend upon us again, was very happy with the generous salary he'd been paid. He never knew that the forty-nine percent of the stock that he thought he owned, I had been paying to the KSLT employees.''

"Isn't that illegal?'' John asked.

"Not really.'' She smiled slyly. "He signed all the papers.''

"Ohmygod,'' Margaret breathed out. Larceny ran amok in Rachel's family.

"So, as we bury my poor brother, Sid, which we'll broadcast live at five o'clock tonight—after all, this is still a sweeps period—I'm sure he'd be happy to know that KSLT is forty-nine percent employee owned.''

Silence greeted the announcement. Mouths had dropped open, eyes were as glazed as the half-eaten doughnuts.

"Maybe I should take my box of Sid commemorative golf balls and put them on my fireplace mantel at home,'' Willie said. "If I had a fireplace.''

"Sid would have liked that. He always wanted his balls to hang in a place of honor,'' Rachel said.

Chen held up his box of golf balls. "I was going to suggest we all head out to the links and take a few whacks at Sid's face, but I kind of think that I'll set these babies on my mantel, too.''

Someone else waved a box in the air. "Thanks, buddy. Sorry for everything I called you in the past.'' That sentiment brought murmurs of agreement rippling through the crowd.

Margaret's smile was bittersweet. Sid, wherever he was, was finally getting the respect he'd craved. She slipped out the door and headed toward her office.

John watched Maggie sneak out of the room and knew he had no choice but to go after her.

The past few days had been the worst in his life. He didn't know where everything between them had gone wrong. He mentally reran the events leading up to her announcement, and something didn't ring true. But he didn't know what.

"Maggie,'' he called out. "Wait.'' He didn't realize how

terrified he'd been that she'd ignore him, until she stopped, and he found himself feeling overwhelming relief.

He expected her eyes to be filled with self-righteous independence, that get-out-of-my face look he had come to know and admire. Instead, the baby blues staring at him were filled with remorse. He only had one question. "Why?"

She looked down, then looked at him again. "You need to follow your dream."

"You are my dream."

She shook her head in determined denial. "Peter Jennings."

He reached out for her, but she backed away. "Come here."

She kept backing up, shaking her head. "I can't."

"Maggie, *you* are what I want."

This time she moved toward him, her hand extended, until she was almost standing on his toes. She caressed his cheek, his chin, and finally outlined the shape of his lips. "You didn't tell me you were offered that job in New York. The job you've wanted forever."

"Is that what this is all about?"

She nodded.

"It's only a job, no big—"

She wouldn't let him finish, silencing him with a finger across his mouth.

"You've waited years for that job. You've finally got the big boys coming after you, offering you the one thing you've worked your whole life for. You had no right to refuse that job because I want, I need, to stay here. You can't change your whole future because my needs are different than yours."

"Are you finished?"

She nodded. "For now anyway."

He backed her against the wall, covering her with his body, relishing the fact that he was once again touching her. God, how he'd missed her. "I don't know if I can

explain this right. It's jumbled up inside. But I've been
thinking about what's important. And what's not.''

Her expression looked so heartbroken. He wanted to
carry her off and make love to her forever.

''Look at our differences.'' He tried his best to explain.
''I'm a GED graduate. You're Rice. No one would take a
chance on me. Except Sid. Everyone wants you. Now, even
the CBS affiliate in Houston, where you've been trying for
five years to get a job, wants you.''

He pushed away from the wall, and paced. Suddenly he
needed to place some distance between them. ''So I had
this dream that someday I would be another Peter Jennings.
That I would make it to the big time.''

''Your dream came true.''

''No, it didn't. My dream changed in New York. I realized that being offered the job was very important. Being
with you was more important.''

''Really?'' she asked softly, as if not quite believing him.

''So now I have a dilemma. What do I do?''

''What?''

''I make a list. What's important, what's more important.
It was important to me to prove that I'm worthy of you.''

''I always thought you were worthy,'' Maggie blurted.

''No, you didn't,'' he said.

''Yes, I did. And as a worthy man, you'll have to take
the job,'' Maggie said.

''I'm not taking the job. Because what's important in my
life is *you,* not New York, not Peter Jennings, not Julie's
offer. Just *you.*''

''And what's important to me is that you go to New York
and fulfill your dream. Because let me tell you something,
John Patrick Hennessey—'' her finger pointed into his
chest ''—you're acting all romantic and love struck now,
but in two months, or six months, or maybe a year, it'll
sink in what you let pass you by, and then you won't love
me. You'll hate me. And you'll always blame me for staying in Sugar Land, and not moving to New York so that

you could follow your dream.'' She dropped her hand and hurried away from him.

''That's not true,'' he shouted after her.

John shoved his hands in his pockets, feeling the soft velvet Tiffany's box, holding on to it for dear life. He watched as Maggie turned the corner, going out of his sight. Damn, that woman was stubborn.

NOVEMBER 27 AT 10:55 p.m. Margaret counted down the minutes leading up to the last broadcast of the last day of the month-long sweeps period. The commercials would soon end and she sat in her usual chair waiting for Hennessey to come back from wherever he had wandered off to this time. Her hands clenched tightly around her pencil, her eyes hurt. She was more than ready for the month to end.

Hennessey might not realize this now, but someday he'd thank her for insisting he give New York a try. She couldn't worry about that right now though. Now she had more immediate problems.

Margaret had refused to get married on the six o'clock news, despite the fact that the wedding had been arranged, and family and friends began arriving at the studio around four that afternoon. Even Linda the flight attendant came, and Julie brought the vice president of news with her. Essie ran around arranging flowers, dangling all Margaret's jewels, driving the sound men crazy.

Hennessey begged her to reconsider, but she refused to budge. She knew what was best—he needed to go back to New York, and fulfill his dream.

But the man was like a pit bull, determined to get what he wanted in the end, and what he wanted was her.

So what did he do? Right there, at the very end of the six o'clock news, that scoundrel told the viewers to stay tuned to the eleven o'clock news, and the wedding would take place then. Then Hennessey turned and winked at her, which was totally unfair, since he knew she was a sucker for his winks.

Didn't he understand she couldn't marry him for his own good? There wasn't going to be a wedding, not at eleven, not ever.

Her mother had ordered a catered dinner from LaViere's for the hundreds of people filling up the studio. "It's not over until it's over, dear," Myrna had said, pinching Margaret's cheek.

"It's not going to happen," Margaret told her.

As the evening wore on, no one seemed inclined to leave. These people really didn't take a hint. Margaret sat at her anchor desk surrounded by the cloying scent of bridal flowers that had been used to decorate the set.

A huge wedding bouquet of lily of the valley and pink tea roses sat on her lap, their sweet fragrance wafting toward her, reminding her—as it should have reminded the rest of this sorry group—that the wedding wasn't going to take place. This day had proven to be nothing more than a total waste of time and money.

The minister refused the dinner and waited patiently out in the wings. He was one stubborn man. How many times did she have to tell him there would be no wedding? He only smiled benevolently upon her.

Willie held on to his camcorder, and the two cameramen who had been hired to work the new cameras Rachel had bought signaled that they'd finished setting up for the eleven o'clock news.

At exactly 10:59, the studio door flew open. The familiar sound of Hennessey's shoes running up to the set made her throat catch. Then she saw he had the minister in tow.

"What did you bring him in here for?" Margaret demanded.

"Sorry," he mumbled as he sat down. "The guy looked lonely."

"He wasn't lonely. It's all an act."

Hennessey placed the earphone in his ear. Chen began his countdown, "Five, four, three, two, one, blastoff."

Margaret and Hennessey reported the news. The weatherman and sportscaster Rachel had hired finished their reports. Only two more minutes of commercials left, then they'd do their "In Your Face" commentary and the sweeps month would finally be over. She couldn't wait.

The camera locked on Hennessey as he started, "A week or so ago, Maggie gave me the honor of allowing me to call her Maggie. She only lets special people call her that. Her students." He looked at her. "You didn't know I knew about the students, did you?"

She shook her head and her bottom lip began to quiver.

"As well as some very special women whose lives she's helped get back together. You didn't know I knew about them, either, huh, Maggie?"

Again she shook her head, but this time tears spilled from her eyes and fell down her cheeks.

"Before we left for New York, Maggie had done this wonderful 'In Your Face' commentary about birds flying to earth, getting splattered and going to heaven. Do you remember that, Maggie?"

"I'm sure everyone does." She smiled in the camera. "One of my finest moments."

Hennessey pulled a small velvet box from his breast pocket and opened the lid. The diamond hit the lights and almost blinded her.

"Maggie," he said. "About ten days ago, Sid planned a wedding for us. He ordered the minister and the flowers. I have a feeling that your mother had something to do with the overabundance of guests and reporters crowding this studio, and that delicious French dinner we all had."

She nodded, and felt her face grow warm. She used her fingertips to wipe her tears.

"What Sid didn't plan was for me to fall so madly, deeply, passionately in love with you that no matter how

you try to run me off, for what you think is my own good,
I'm not going anywhere.''

Her voice was teary. ''You'll never forgive me if you
don't take the job in New York.''

He placed the ring on her finger. ''I bought this in New
York. After I got the offer.''

''After?'' she asked, her voice filled with wonder.

''Getting the offer meant the world to me. Taking the
job means nothing.'' He stood and pulled her up with him,
crushing white and pink petals between them. His mouth
descended on hers, stroking, probing, until she opened to
him, letting all the magic that was Hennessey take over.
He lifted his hands to her face, cupping both cheeks, and
slowly broke the kiss. ''You're important.'' His voice
sounded rough, husky. ''You're my life.'' He took her
hand. ''Come with me.''

He walked her over to where the wedding designers had
made the set look like a chapel. ''I love you madly, Mag-
gie-o-mine.''

''Hennessey.'' She lifted her gaze to his face. He looked
happy—at peace—and a little nervous. ''Are you sure?''

''I've never been more sure about anything in my life.''

The minister glanced at his watch and said, ''Come, children. Everyone's been waiting a-a-a-a-a-a-ll night.''

Family and friends moved onto the set and surrounded
the couple. The cameras rolled.

''Dearly beloved,'' the minister began. ''We have waited
a long, long time tonight to finally witness this event. Any
longer and it would be tomorrow. Therefore, it is with great
relief and much pleasure I say, we are gathered here this
evening to finally join together this man and this
woman…''

Epilogue

One Year Later

AROUND THE TOWN
with Matilda Mae Tuttle
GIGI MAKES AN ENTRANCE

Last night, November 27, on Margaret and John's first wedding anniversary, Sugar Land's KSLT, for the second year in a row, cemented its position as the number-one Houston area television station in the six and eleven time periods. Our town's favorite married couple delivered what is sure to be the most memorable newscast in KSLT history.

Halfway through the 6:00 p.m. broadcast, a very pregnant Margaret smiled into the cameras, and stated, "It's time." Who would have thought that big, strong hubby John would fall off his chair in a dead faint?

Dr. W. Griffin Scott, Sugar Land's new trauma surgeon who was touring KSLT at the time, revived the expectant father, and declared him fit enough to travel in the ambulance with Margaret to Sugar Land General.

Five hours later, in time for the 11:00 p.m. news—what troopers these people are—this reporter was lead into the Hennessey's private hospital suite. There, surrounded by the couple's closest friends and relatives, John, quite the baritone, sang, "Thank Heaven for Little Girls," as he handed out pink cigars. Margaret cuddled her little bundle of joy as she gazed at her husband with love.

Welcome to Sugar Land, Texas, Leslie Caron Hennessey. How absolutely adorable that your parents have nicknamed you Gigi.

And you read it here first, folks!

Take 2 bestselling love stories FREE

Plus get a FREE surprise gift!

Special Limited-Time Offer

Mail to Harlequin Reader Service®

3010 Walden Avenue
P.O. Box 1867
Buffalo, N.Y. 14240-1867

YES! Please send me 2 free Harlequin Love & Laughter™ novels and my free surprise gift. Then send me 4 brand-new novels every other month, which I will receive months before they appear in bookstores. Bill me at the low price of $2.90 each plus 25¢ delivery per book and applicable sales tax if any*. That's the complete price, and a saving of over 10% off the cover prices—quite a bargain! I understand that accepting the books and gift places me under no obligation ever to buy any books. I can always return a shipment and cancel at any time. Even if I never buy another book from Harlequin, the 2 free books and the surprise gift are mine to keep forever.

102 HEN CH7N

Name _____ (PLEASE PRINT)

Address _____ Apt. No. _____

City _____ State _____ Zip _____

This offer is limited to one order per household and not valid to present Love & Laughter™ subscribers. *Terms and prices are subject to change without notice. Sales tax applicable in N.Y.

ULL-98   ©1996 Harlequin Enterprises Limited

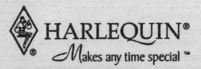

Don't miss these Harlequin favorites by some of our bestselling authors!

HT#25721	THE ONLY MAN IN WYOMING	$3.50 U.S. ☐	
	by Kristine Rolofson	$3.99 CAN. ☐	
HP#11869	WICKED CAPRICE	$3.50 U.S. ☐	
	by Anne Mather	$3.99 CAN. ☐	
HR#03438	ACCIDENTAL WIFE	$3.25 U.S. ☐	
	by Day Leclaire	$3.75 CAN. ☐	
HS#70737	STRANGERS WHEN WE MEET	$3.99 U.S. ☐	
	by Rebecca Winters	$4.50 CAN. ☐	
HI#22405	HERO FOR HIRE	$3.75 U.S. ☐	
	by Laura Kenner	$4.25 CAN. ☐	
HAR#16673	ONE HOT COWBOY	$3.75 U.S. ☐	
	by Cathy Gillen Thacker	$4.25 CAN. ☐	
HH#28952	JADE	$4.99 U.S. ☐	
	by Ruth Langan	$5.50 CAN. ☐	
LL#44005	STUCK WITH YOU	$3.50 U.S. ☐	
	by Vicki Lewis Thompson	$3.99 CAN. ☐	

(limited quantities available on certain titles)

AMOUNT	$ _____
POSTAGE & HANDLING	$ _____
($1.00 for one book, 50¢ for each additional)	
APPLICABLE TAXES*	$ _____
TOTAL PAYABLE	$ _____
(check or money order—please do not send cash)	

To order, complete this form and send it, along with a check or money order for the total above, payable to Harlequin Books, to: **In the U.S.:** 3010 Walden Avenue, P.O. Box 9047, Buffalo, NY 14269-9047; **In Canada:** P.O. Box 613, Fort Erie, Ontario, L2A 5X3.

Name: _____

Address: _____ City: _____

State/Prov.: _____ Zip/Postal Code: _____

Account Number (if applicable): _____

*New York residents remit applicable sales taxes.
Canadian residents remit applicable GST and provincial taxes.

Look us up on-line at: http://www.romance.net

HBLAJ98

HARLEQUIN ULTIMATE GUIDES™

A series of how-to books for today's woman.

Act now to order some of these extremely
helpful guides just for you!

*Whatever the situation, Harlequin Ultimate Guides™
has all the answers!*

#80507	HOW TO TALK TO A	$4.99 U.S. ☐
	NAKED MAN	$5.50 CAN. ☐
#80508	I CAN FIX THAT	$5.99 U.S. ☐
		$6.99 CAN. ☐
#80510	WHAT YOUR TRAVEL AGENT	$5.99 U.S. ☐
	KNOWS THAT YOU DON'T	$6.99 CAN. ☐
#80511	RISING TO THE OCCASION	
	More Than Manners: Real Life	$5.99 U.S. ☐
	Etiquette for Today's Woman	$6.99 CAN. ☐
#80513	WHAT GREAT CHEFS	$5.99 U.S. ☐
	KNOW THAT YOU DON'T	$6.99 CAN. ☐
#80514	WHAT SAVVY INVESTORS	$5.99 U.S. ☐
	KNOW THAT YOU DON'T	$6.99 CAN. ☐
#80509	GET WHAT YOU WANT OUT OF	$5.99 U.S. ☐
	LIFE—AND KEEP IT!	$6.99 CAN. ☐

(quantities may be limited on some titles)

TOTAL AMOUNT	$
POSTAGE & HANDLING	$
($1.00 for one book, 50¢ for each additional)	
APPLICABLE TAXES*	$ _____
TOTAL PAYABLE	$ _____

(check or money order—please do not send cash)

To order, complete this form and send it, along with a check or money
order for the total above, payable to Harlequin Ultimate Guides, to:
In the U.S.: 3010 Walden Avenue, P.O. Box 9047, Buffalo, NY
14269-9047; **In Canada:** P.O. Box 613, Fort Erie, Ontario, L2A 5X3.

Name: _____

Address: _____ City: _____

State/Prov.: _____ Zip/Postal Code: _____

*New York residents remit applicable sales taxes.
Canadian residents remit applicable GST and provincial taxes.

◈ HARLEQUIN®

Look us up on-line at: http://www.romance.net

HNFBL4

MEN at WORK

All work and no play?
Not these men!

July 1998

MACKENZIE'S LADY by Dallas Schulze

Undercover agent Mackenzie Donahue's
lazy smile and deep blue eyes were his best
weapons. But after rescuing—and kissing!—
damsel in distress Holly Reynolds, how could
he betray her by spying on her brother?

August 1998

MISS LIZ'S PASSION by Sherryl Woods

Todd Lewis could put up a building with ease,
but quailed at the sight of a classroom! Still,
Liz Gentry, his son's teacher, was no battle-ax,
and soon Todd started planning some
extracurricular activities of his own....

September 1998

A CLASSIC ENCOUNTER
by Emilie Richards

Doctor Chris Matthews was intelligent, sexy
and *very* good with his hands—which made
him all the more dangerous to single mom
Lizette St. Hilaire. So how long could she
resist Chris's special brand of TLC?

Available at your favorite retail outlet!

MEN AT WORK™

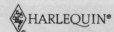 

Look us up on-line at: http://www.romance.net

PMAW2